A CLOSER LOOK

A Closer Look

Iron Horse Mystery #5

C.J. Shane

Published by Rope's End Publishing

ISBN 978-1-951524-33-3

Typesetting services by BOOKOW.COM

Acknowledgments

Sincere thanks go to Tucson graphic designer Lynne East-Itkin for the book cover design, and to Dawn Lewis of County Durham, England, for editorial services. And thanks to my beta readers, too.

Letty Valdez Mysteries

Desert Jade 2017
Dragon's Revenge 2018
Daemon Waters 2019
Direct Evidence 2022

Cat Miranda Mysteries

Kissed 2020
Fair Play 2021
The Broken Pot 2022

Iron Horse Mysteries

Take Four #1 2023
Shadow Man #2 2023
In the Slips #3 2024
Clouds #4 2024
A Closer Look #5 2024

CONTENTS

1 An Accidental Meeting

Logan Reid woke up suddenly, his body tense. He could hear the sound of gunshots not far away. Too close for comfort. Too close to the apartments that he managed, Casa Pacifica. "Shit," he muttered to himself. His wife, Zoey, was curled up against him, still asleep. Logan carefully edged himself away from her, rose to his feet, and quickly pulled on a t-shirt and jeans. He went into his living room, closing the bedroom door behind him.

He looked out of the big front window of his apartment, where he immediately saw a young man staggering in the street, a gun in his hand. The man clumsily lifted his arm into the air and shot the gun again. Logan heard another sound, this time coming from the hallway. Chito. He could hear Chito Alvarez, a detective with the Tucson Police Department, leaving his apartment and heading toward the front door of the building.

Logan opened his door just as Chito passed him.

"Call 911, Logan," Chito said. "Tell them I'm here and that I told you to call."

Logan nodded, returned to his apartment, found his phone and did as Chito instructed. He followed Chito out of the building into the front yard.

"Drop the gun!" Chito shouted at the young man. Logan could see that, despite being shirtless and wearing only pajama bottoms, Chito was standing with his legs apart and with both hands on his service gun, now pointed at the young man. He was a cop ready to shoot.

The young man began singing, struggling to stay on his feet. To Logan, he looked drunk or stoned or both.

"*Ain't no sunshine when she's gone*," the young man sobbed.

"Chito, I know him," Logan said in a low voice. "He's a former student of mine. Let me try talking to him."

Chito shook his head. "This is dangerous, Logan."

"I called like you said. The cops are on their way," Logan answered. He stepped to Chito's side. "Darren, remember me? You were in my introductory philosophy class."

The young man focused on Logan. "Oh, yeah, Mr. Reid. I liked your class." He began singing again. "*Ain't no sunshine when she's gon*e."

"I have a song for you, Darren. But you have to put the gun down first."

"I like songs." He staggered forward. "Mr. Reid, my girl dumped me."

"Put the gun down, and I'll sing you a tune."

The young man, Darren, leaned forward, almost lost his balance, but he was able to place the gun onto the street pavement.

Chito moved quickly to take possession of the gun.

"Okay, here we go," Logan said. "I can't sing for shit so be patient. One of the lyrics is something like 'you don't have a girl to make you smile,' and every verse ends with this." And Logan took a deep breath and sang, "*Don't worry. Be happy.*"

"I can't be happy, Mr. Reid." Darren sobbed again. "She's gone."

"Darren, we all have our struggles. Do you remember meeting my wife Caroline?"

Darren nodded. "She was sweet to me."

"She died several years ago."

"Oh! That's so sad." Darren began crying again.

Logan stepped forward and hugged the young man. "I survived. My life now is good. You'll survive, and you'll find another girl to love." He could hear the cops coming, sirens on.

Chito stepped forward. "Darren, looks like you've had too much to drink. Or did you take some drugs?"

"I don't know. My friend gave me a pill, and he said to wash it down with the tequila."

"What was the pill?" Chito asked.

"I don't know." He turned to Logan. "Do you think I'll ever find a girl who will love me?"

"Yes, definitely. Just let go of this painful episode, and be open to new possibilities," Logan answered.

"Do you have a new possibility, Mr. Reid?" Darren was weaving on his feet.

"Yes, her name is Zoey."

"Oh, that's so sweet." Darren began sobbing again.

A cop car pulled up. The siren and lights were turned off now, and a cop got out of the police car.

"Chito, can you please tell Darren what's going to happen now?" Logan asked.

"Darren, my officer is going to take you in and put you in a cell until you sober up."

Darren nodded. "I need to sober up. I drank too much. I guess I goofed up."

"Yes, but it could have been worse. Time to go with my officer." Chito gestured to the officer who was carrying handcuffs.

"Okay." Darren turned to the cop. Logan could hear him singing, "*Don't worry. Be happy*" as the cop took him away and put him in the backseat of the police car.

Chito turned to Logan. "Thanks for the help, but you know that could have gone bad really quickly."

"Yeah, I know. But he's a good kid, and I didn't want you to have to shoot him."

Chito nodded. "I think I'll go back to bed now."

"Me, too."

They returned together to the ground floor of Casa Pacifica. There was a woman standing in the hallway. Chito didn't know her.

"Everything's okay," Logan said. "We can all go back to bed now, Remedios."

The woman smiled and said, "Okay, I'll do that." But instead of turning to go, she took a good look at Chito, his shirtless chest and his pajama bottoms. There were cartoon Minions making funny faces printed on the pajamas.

"Nice pajamas." She grinned.

Chito frowned. "My daughter gave these to me for my birthday."

"Okay, back to bed. See you boys tomorrow." Remedios turned and walked away.

"Have a good sleep in those pajamas, Chito. So cute!" Logan snickered.

"Shut up, Logan." Chito growled.

Logan laughed out loud as he closed his door behind him.

Chito went into his apartment and fell into bed.

* * *

Chito Alvarez opened the door of his refrigerator to see if there was anything else he could put in this large tossed salad. He'd started with lettuce, then added cherry tomatoes cut in half, then grated carrots, and chopped peppers. He found a couple of just-ripe avocados, peeled and chopped them, and added them to the salad. Then some shredded mozzarella cheese. He sighed. He didn't like to cook, but he felt an obligation to take something to the group Sunday evening potluck. No one complained about his salads. And a big salad didn't require a recipe or actual "cooking."

Suddenly, there was a loud squealing sound outside. He felt a flash of alarm course through him. He turned to peer out the window of his apartment to the side yard where his daughter Isabel and Charlie, son of the apartment manager Logan Reid, were playing together. Squeals transformed into giggles as the two almost six-year-olds chased a greyhound dog in a big circle. Charlie quickly changed directions, Isabel followed, and now the dog, Gwenny, that was her name, was chasing the two kids.

Chito sighed. Relax, he told himself. They're just being noisy kids, having fun. Being a Tucson cop for the past twelve years meant that every time he heard a sudden noise, Chito would feel that same burst of alarm. He needed to learn to relax or he was going to end up with some stress-related health problem. "Shit," he muttered to himself. He thought about that song that Logan had sung really early this morning. Chito wondered if he'd ever stop worrying and be happy. His job came with built-in stress.

And his daughter. He loved Isabel more than he thought possible. Above all, he wanted her to be safe, and at the same time, he didn't want to smother her. She need some space to play with Charlie and Gwenny, and making squealing sounds was part of her play. Isabel was having fun, and that's good, he told himself. Let her be.

Chito turned back to the salad, decided he was done, so he slid it onto a refrigerator shelf. He shook his head and frowned. He'd done more food prep since he moved into Casa Pacifica Apartments than he'd ever done in his life. Most of the time, he just stopped off at a local restaurant for carry-out, or maybe went by a food truck and got a quick meal. He frequently ate at his desk in his office at Tucson Police Department headquarters, or he ate at home alone. Since Isabel spent all week with her mom and her step-dad and half-siblings, he only had to provide meals for her on the weekends. And sometimes not even then.

But now, everything had changed. Every Sunday evening, he joined the other residents of Casa Pacifica Apartments to eat together and to have a good time at the weekly potluck dinner. He was surprised at how much he really enjoyed these group potlucks. The residents were all very amiable and supportive of his work. But he didn't really enjoy messing with the food prep. He was going to have to think about that. Either really learn how to cook and enjoy it, or start buying something to bring to the potlucks. But what? He looked at the clock. Residents would meet at Logan and Zoey's apartment for the potluck in a couple of hours.

Suddenly, another loud sound interrupted his thoughts, but this time it wasn't a squeal but more of a scream. Again, that instant burst of alarm went through him. Chito looked out and saw Isabel sitting on the ground crying. He quickly turned and ran from his apartment, slamming the door behind him, and he arrived at Isabel's side in less than ten seconds. Isabel was sobbing now.

"What happened?" Chito asked, kneeling next to Isabel.

Charlie spoke first. "Isabel fell. She skidded on the gravel over there and landed her knees." Chito looked at Charlie and nodded. He could see that Charlie had a very distressed look on his face.

Chito could see that there were scrapes on both of Isabel's knees, but one knee was especially injured. Blood was dripping down her leg, and Chito could see bits of dirt and pebbles in the wound.

"It hurts, Daddy." Isabel sobbed again.

Gwenny came forward and tried to lick Isabel's face.

"Charlie, hold on to Gweeny. I have to take Isabel inside," Chito said.

"Can I help?"

The sound of a woman's voice startled Chito. He looked up. She was very close to him, and he hadn't even noticed her. Too focused on Isabel. "She scraped her knees. I'm taking her in."

Chito realized that the woman was the same one he'd seen really early that morning, the one who had complimented his cartoon pajama bottoms. Remedios. Yeah, that was her name.

The woman knelt down next to them. She spoke directly to Isabel in a soft, comforting voice, a smile on her face. "What's your name, sweetie?"

"Isabel." She pointed to her knee. "It hurts."

"Let me take a closer look." The woman knelt down next to Isabel. She was facing Chito now. "I think we can fix this, Isabel."

Chito frowned. Okay, she was trying to be nice, but she was being sort of intrusive. Who the hell was she? He didn't really know her. And where had she come from? "You don't have to do this. I'll take care of her," he said firmly.

The woman looked at Chito and smiled. "I'm sure you can take care of her. But I'm a nurse practitioner, and I have several years' experience working in my hospital's emergency room. Taking care of Isabel and people like her is what I do."

"Oh," Chito said, surprised. A nurse practitioner was up the hierarchy from a regular registered nurse, closer to a doctor. And with emergency room experience. "Okay. What should we do? And who are you?"

"I'm Remedios Davila. Remember me from early this morning? You live here, right?"

"Yes. I remember you. I'm Chito Alvarez, and this is my daughter Isabel."

"And I'm Charlie. Isabel is my friend," Charlie added.

Remedios smiled again. "I suggest you take Isabel to your apartment. I'll join you in a minute with supplies." She stood and walked back up the front stairs and into Casa Pacifica Apartments, disappearing quickly.

Chito picked up Isabel and cradled her in his arms. "Come on, Charlie. Let's go in. Bring Gwenny. But you'll have to make her sit and behave."

"I will. I promise," Charlie said.

Two minutes later, they were back in Chito's apartment. He'd just placed Isabel on a chair when there was a knock on his door. "Charlie, go open the door for me, please." Charlie complied.

Remedios Davila entered the apartment with a smile on her face. She was carrying a leather bag, similar to what Chito thought of as a doctor's medical bag. She pulled up a chair and sat facing Isabel.

"Here's what we're going to do. First, I'm going to put to sleep the hurt in your knee. Your daddy is going to put a towel over your face while you are holding your breath. Do you know how to hold your breath?"

So calm. So professional. Chito was grateful that Remedios had appeared.

"Yes, I know how to hold my breath," Isabel said, her voice trembling.

"Chito, do you have a little towel?"

He stood and found a clean, folded dish towel in his kitchen.

Remedios pulled a spray bottle of topical anesthetic from her bag. "When I say 'go,' we're all going to hold our breath. And your daddy is going to put the towel over your face."

"Me, too? Can I hold my breath, too?" Charlie asked. He giggled.

"Yes. All of us. Not the dog, though." Remedios looked at Chito and wiggled her eyebrows. "You, too, Chito."

Chito smiled. Calm, professional, and charming, too.

"Ready?" Everyone nodded.

"Okay. One...Two...Three. Go!"

All four of them took a deep breath and held it. Chito quickly placed the towel over his daughter's face just as Remedios sprayed the topical anesthetic onto her injured knee. She turned and made a gesture to Chito to remove the towel.

"Great! We can breathe again!"

"It doesn't hurt anymore," Isabel said, surprise in her voice.

"Not for a while. It will hurt again, and then it will hurt less, and then less, and then it will stop hurting altogether. I'm going to clean your wound now, and put an antibiotic cream on it." Remedios proceeded to do just that.

Chito watched. Finally he said, "What do you think about the wound? What should I do?"

"It's painful but not really a deep wound, just a nasty scrape. You'll need to watch it and make sure that no signs of infection appear."

"Okay. I'll tell her mother. She and I are divorced, and I only have Isabel on the weekends."

"Tell her mom to watch for any pain, inflammation, redness, or swelling, which is an early sign of infection. I'll give you some antibiotic cream to give to her."

Chito nodded. "I'll follow your instructions."

Remedios stood. "It was nice meeting you all."

Chito stood. "I don't know how to thank you."

"My pleasure. Like I said, this is what I do." She smiled again, turned, and headed toward the door.

"Wait. Please," Chito said. He wanted to know more about her. "Are you staying here?"

"Yes, I quit my job at the hospital where I worked in Texas, and I've returned to Tucson to live. I'm looking for a new job now. I'm staying with my sister, Frida."

"Frida?" Chito was surprised. Remedios was nothing like Frida, the union strike leader who was something of a hell raiser, and who had been arrested five times.

"Yes, Frida. She's my big sister. Half-sister really, because we have different dads. I'm staying with her until I find a new job and an apartment of my own."

"Oh," Chito said, at a loss for words now. Remedios was nothing, nothing, nothing like Frida. She was calm and competent and reassuring…and very pretty. Dark, shoulder-length hair, big brown eyes, a dimple in one cheek when she smiled. Lovely. He blurted out, "You're not like Frida."

Remedios laughed. "No. We're different for sure. But we get along well." By this time, she was half-way out the door. She turned back and said, "So I'll see you at the potluck?"

"Oh, yeah, the potluck. We'll be there."

Remedios waved at everyone and left Chito's apartment, closing the door behind her.

Chito turned to the two children. "Okay, Isabel. Looks like you are in better shape now. How about if we find something for you two to do that is a little calmer?"

"Can we watch TV?" Charlie asked. "My daddy lets me watch TV sometimes."

Chito smiled. He knew from talking to Logan that Charlie's access to the television was restricted, and he wasn't allowed to have any digital devices at all. Logan had opinions about that sort of thing.

"Okay. You can watch the PBS Kids channel." Chito turned on the TV.

"Yippie!" Charlie said. "*Nature Cat* is coming on now. I love *Nature Cat*."

"I love *Nature Cat*, too." Isabel sat down on the sofa in front of the television. Charlie and Gwenny joined them on the sofa.

Chito sighed with relief as the two children became caught up in *Nature Cat*'s story. He could see that the animated cartoon story featured a big yellow cat with a purple nose that became a backyard explorer as soon as his humans left home for work everyday. Logan would approve.

After about twenty minutes of *Nature Cat*, Chito heard a soft knock at his door. He opened the door and found Logan Reid standing there.

"Hey, Logan. Come on in."

"No, thanks. I'm just here for a minute. We just got back from the market. Is it okay for Charlie to stay with you until it's time for you to come to our place? Zoey and I need to make something for us to contribute to the potluck."

"Sure. They were playing outside with the dog, and now they're watching the PBS Kids' channel."

"Has Charlie been good?"

"Very good. He and Isabel get along great."

"Okay. Then we'll see you at the potluck." Logan turned to go.

* * *

Chito managed to carry his large salad bowl and a couple of bottles of salad dressing safely to the potluck, all while herding two rambunctious kids and a big dog in front of him. Lucky for him, Logan and Zoey's apartment door was just a few feet away. Logan directed Chito to put the salad on the long dinner table, already set with dinner plates, wine glasses, and several other dishes.

He put his salad bowl with the other dishes, then looked around the room. Zoey, Logan's wife, was in the kitchen stirring something on the stove. Seated around the room were other Casa Pacifica residents: veterinarian Angela and photographer Marc who lived together upstairs; artist Xochi and chef Li who also lived upstairs. Chito knew Xochi and Li were a couple, but he wasn't sure who lived where. Frida, the other downstairs resident, wasn't present. But Remedios Davila was there. Remedios, Frida's half sister; Remedios, the nurse practitioner who had treated his daughter with loving kindness; Remedios with the one dimple. She smiled and waved at him. Chito returned her smile. He felt himself getting warm.

The dinner was just as Chito had come to expect. Good food and plenty of it. Lots of joking and laughter. He was glad he lived here. For the moment, he could forget about his work, despite what had happened early this morning. The days with his daughter Isabel and these potluck dinners were a real stress relief, often with moments of real happiness.

The meal finished, dishes were cleared away and were being washed. Logan was with the children in Charlie's bedroom. Chito could hear the kids giggling and enthusiastically demanding to see another *Nature Cat* episode, and after a moment's pause, Logan agreed. He soon returned to the adults, and everyone gathered together in front of the living room's big window, all sitting on the sofa or stuffed chairs nearby.

Logan spoke first. "I don't have much to tell. My classes at the community college are going well, mainly because I have a good group of students this semester. It's early November, and Charlie's birthday is coming up. Zoey and I are talking about how to celebrate it. He's going to be six. That's a big deal, so we want to make the birthday special. How about you, Zoey?" He reached out and took her hand.

"At the end of this semester, I'm going on leave from my teaching job at the high school," Zoey said. "And …" She stood up and thrust her stomach and belly out so that her state of pregnancy was obvious. "…I'm getting bigger by the minute. As I told you last week, Logan did a number on me, and now I'm carrying twins!" She laughed.

"I did a number on you?" Logan's eyebrows went up and a smile grew on his face. Everyone laughed.

"Boys or girls or one of each?" Angela asked.

"The doctor thinks one is a boy, but she's not sure about the other baby." Zoey sat down. "I'm happy." She turned to Angela. "What have you been up to?"

"Things are going well at the veterinary clinic. This week we managed to save a family dog that had been run over. But, unfortunately, he has only three legs now. And we took in a female Golden Retriever in the last stage of pregnancy. She gave birth and now has twelve pups."

"Whoa. That's a lot," Xochi said.

"And how can she feed so many?" Li asked.

"It is a lot," Angela said. "We're helping her with the feedings." She turned to Marc and smiled.

"I'm getting work ready for an exhibit that will be held in a big art photography gallery in Phoenix. That will be after Christmas. And I'm doing some volunteer work for an animal rescue organization that Angela told me about. I take photos of the animals, mostly dogs and cats, that show their big, sad eyes. The idea is to make them look lovable and sweet and lonely so they will be adopted."

"You're the sweet one, Marco, my love," Angela said. She kissed him.

Logan spoke now. "Frida is off organizing some grocery workers. I think she said she's out in California. You've all met Remedios, Frida's sister?" Everyone nodded.

"Hi, everyone. I'm busy looking for a job now," Remedios said.

"Am I the only one here that sees the connection between Frida and Remedios?" Xochi said. She looked around the room.

"They're sisters," Logan answered.

Xochi made a face. "Anyone ever take an art history class?" she asked impatiently.

Chito noticed that Remedios was grinning. "I always wondered if Frida was named after Frida Kahlo, that famous Mexican artist," he said.

"Exactly. Very good, Chito," Xochi said. "And Remedios?"

No one said anything.

"Oh, you are all hopeless. Remedios Varo!"

"Tell us about Remedios Varo," Zoey said.

"She was a Spanish artist who left Spain, went to France, and then she fled France when the Nazis took over. She ended up in Mexico and lived there the rest of her life. She was a surrealist painter."

Remedios was nodding her head again and grinning.

"Okay, so none of us knows much about art history. Sorry about that, Xochi," Logan smiled. "I understand that you and Li have a big announcement."

Xochi and Li jumped up, holding hands and grinning.

"You already know about Li and his food truck gig. That's going really great! And here's what's new. We're opening an art gallery and a music venue!" Xochi said. Her voice was full of excitement.

"That's right," Li added. He was grinning and sounded just as excited as Xochi. "We bought that old laundromat next to the market a few blocks from here."

"We had enough money to do that because we sold that Chinese scroll and several other antique books my grandfather left me," Xochi added.

Li continued, "That gave us the money both to buy the building and remodel it. We've been working on the upgrades since the summer."

"The big front room will be the art gallery." Xochi grinned.

"We'll get to see Xochi's work and sometimes other artists," Li added.

"The back room will be my studio. And there's a bathroom, too." Xochi grinned.

"And Xochi can teach classes there. We hired workers to put in a skylight," Li said.

"The gallery will also be a venue for musical events. Solo artists and small groups. Li will be first. He'll play his guitar." Xochi looked up at Li and patted his cheek.

"Yeah." Li looked embarrassed. "Xochi thinks my jazz guitar isn't too bad."

"You're very good!" Xochi put her arms around Li. "Don't forget that!"

Li leaned down and kissed her. "You are very good, too." He wiggled his eyebrows.

"Oh, stop it!" Xochi collapsed into giggles.

"So, who is coming to our opening next Saturday evening?" Li looked around the room.

Logan, Zoey, Angela, and Marc all raised their hands.

"Sounds like a fun date with my man," Zoey said. Logan took her hand and kissed it.

"How about you, Chito?" Li asked. "You can bring a date."

Chito suddenly had a look of dismay on his face. He shook his head. "I'm boring. I work all the time. I don't know any women."

Remedios grinned and said, "Yes, you do. You know me." She stood up. "Chito Alvarez, will you be my date for the opening?"

Chito gasped. "Me? You want me to go with you?"

Everyone laughed.

"Duh," Angela said. She elbowed Chito. "Say yes."

"Uh. Well. Uh. Okay. If you don't mind." Chito looked at Remedios.

She chuckled. "I don't mind. I'll come to your place to pick you up, and we'll walk together to the opening."

Xochi and Li went back to describing all the plans that they had for their new art gallery and music venue. Questions were asked, and answers came quickly and enthusiastically.

Chito sat quietly, not really knowing what to say. It had been a long time since he'd been on a date. A really long time. He suddenly remembered what time it was right now.

"Sorry, folks. I have to take Isabel home now. She has school tomorrow."

Chito called for Isabel, and as they left Logan and Zoey's apartment, everyone waved goodbye.

2 A Cop's Job

Chito took Isabel back to her mother, Juanita, explained the scrape on Isabel's knee, and gave her the tube of antibiotic cream that Remedios had given him. He was grateful that Juanita didn't make a fuss. She took the cream and listened to what he had to say with little comment. He kissed Isabel goodbye and told her he'd see her next weekend.

After a fairly good night's sleep, Chito went to work the next morning. He had no idea of what to expect. That was the life of law enforcement. No telling what crime or crimes might have been committed over the weekend, but it would be his job to figure out what was going on and to apprehend any suspects.

First in was a report by some neighbors on the west side of Tucson. Callers from at least three different homes reported hearing loud yelling, screams, and gunshots from the same home. One person reported that the house was inhabited by a woman with two small children. The woman's name was Vicki Gomez. Chito and Officer Peterson drove to the neighborhood and sat for a few minutes, observing the house where the gunshots had been heard. All was quiet, so the two men went to the door and knocked. No answer. Chito notice that the door wasn't fully closed so he pushed it open and called out.

Suddenly a man appeared from a side door and stood staring at the two cops. He said nothing.

Chito pulled his police identification out of his pocket, held it up, and identified himself. "We understand that there was some kind of conflict here and gunfire was heard. What's going on?"

"Nothing is going on," the man said. "Go away."

Chito noticed that he was young, mid-twenties maybe, white, about five feet, ten inches tall, and scowling at him. Also, he could see that the man was standing at a sideways angle. Chito couldn't see his right lower arm or hand.

"We'd like to see Ms. Gomez. She lives here, right?"

"She's busy. Go away," the man growled.

Chito took a step forward. "We need to see her. Just want to make sure she's okay."

The man swung his right arm up. He was holding a pistol in his right hand. "Go way!" he yelled.

"Put that gun down on the floor and step back!" Chito yelled.

Office Peterson had his gun out now, and Chito reached for his gun in its holster next to his chest under his suit coat.

The young man raised his gun toward the two police officers, and, a second later, he pulled his gun's trigger at the same time that Office Peterson pulled his trigger. Peterson's bullet went into the young man's gut, and he fell to the floor just as his gun's bullet whizzed past Chito, tearing a wound into his upper arm. Then the bullet smashed into Officer Peterson's upper chest near his shoulder, and the cop fell to the ground.

Chito stepped forward and kicked the young man's gun away. He reached down and felt for a pulse. Erratic. The shooter was groaning, only partially conscious. Chito reached into his pocket and called for help from his fellow police officers and for an ambulance. He turned to Officer Peterson.

"How bad is it?"

"Hurts like hell, but I'll survive. I think the bullet maybe broke my collar bone." The policeman frowned. "Shit. I didn't mean to kill him."

"He's still alive. I think he'll make it if we can get him to the hospital ASAP. Keep in mind that if his bullet had landed in your chest a few inches lower, you'd be dead now. You did what you had to do," Chito said. "Help is on the way. I'm going to go inside and see if I can find the woman who lives here." He realized now that he could hear someone crying. A child. No, two children. "Need something to stop the bleeding?" Chito asked.

"No, I have a handkerchief. It doesn't seem to be bleeding much, though. How about you? Is that blood I see?"

"Yeah, just a scratch. I'm going to check on the woman. I'll be back in a minute."

Chito entered the house and went toward the sound of children crying. He found two toddlers, one maybe ten or eleven months old, and the other maybe two years old, both standing up in cribs, both crying their eyes out. There was a woman sprawled out on the floor. He knelt beside the woman and felt for a pulse. She was breathing, but she was unconscious. It was clear to him that she had been badly beaten. There were bruises on her arms, neck and face. Both her eyes were swollen and black. Same with her mouth, swollen with cracked lips. He shook his head and wondered what the hell was wrong with some people to do this to another person, especially a mother of two little kids.

He stood up and called for help again. "We need three ambulances here, one for my officer and one for an abuse victim. We have a wounded perp, too. Also send someone from Arizona Child Safely to help out with two small children."

The next hour was busy. After making sure that both Peterson and the woman, who turned out to be Vicki Gomez, were taken to the hospital, and the shooter, too, Chito made sure the two kids were turned over to the Child Safety representative. Chito returned to police headquarters to report to his chief, Jake Sears.

"Glad to hear Peterson is okay. How about you, Alvarez? Did you get hurt?" Sears asked.

"Just a scratch on my upper arm. I'll be okay."

"Did the medics who came with the ambulance look at you?"

"No, not necessary." Chito did not want to go to the hospital.

Chief Sears frowned. "Alvarez, there's no shame in getting someone to look at you."

Chito paused. He remembered Remedios. Maybe she could look at him.

"Uh...well...I have a friend who is a nurse practitioner. I'll ask her to check me out."

"Do that, Alvarez. And I think you should take a few days off. You've been working a lot lately. You need a break, especially after what happened this morning. Now go home and call that friend of yours."

"Will do." Chito quickly exited the office. He gathered a few things from his desk and headed home. When he arrived and parked his car in the space behind Casa Pacifica, he exited the car and immediately pulled off his suit jacket. A big tear in his blood-soaked shirt sleeve revealed a six-inch long gash in the skin of his upper arm, and probably the muscle, too. Blood was still seeping from the wound. And the wound hurt.

"Shit," he muttered.

Just at that moment, Logan drove up and parked his car. He pulled out a backpack and a small stack of books with him, and he turned to Chito.

"Hey, Chito! How's it going?" Logan stopped and stared at Chito's upper arm. "What happened to you?"

"I kinda got shot."

"Yeah, I can see that. That looks like more than just 'kinda.' Have you seen a doctor?"

"No. I don't like to go to the doctor."

Logan shook his head. "Let's go inside. I'll text Remedios and see if she's here. Maybe she can look at you. She's a nurse practitioner."

Chito nodded. "Yeah, I met her yesterday." He wasn't feeling too great now. Kind of light-headed really.

Together they went to Chito's apartment. Chito tossed his suit jacket aside and removed his holster and gun, which he placed on his desk. Logan retrieved his phone and texted Remedios. Thirty seconds later, his phone beeped.

Logan looked at his phone and then turned to Chito. "Remedios is on her way."

Not long after, Remedios arrived with her medical bag. "What happened?"

"Chito tells me that he 'kinda' got shot," Logan said.

She sat next to Chito. "Let me take a closer look." She frowned. "That's more than 'kinda.' I think your biceps brachii muscle is torn, Chito. Looks like you need some stitches."

"I don't want to go to the hospital." Chito tried to sound professional, but even to his own ears, he sound like a frightened kid.

"You don't have to go to the hospital. I can take care of you. Will you let me take care of you?"

"If you don't mind." He sighed.

"Like I told you, this is my life's work. So, yes, I'll take care of you. First, I want you to go lie down on your sofa. You're looking really pale. Do you feel light-headed?"

"Sort of." Chito saw Remedios glance at Logan who was shaking his head and frowning.

"Do what she says, Chito," Logan said.

"Do you want some water?" Remedios ask.

"Not right now."

"First, let's get that shirt off of you," Remedios said.

Logan helped Chito to move to the sofa, and Remedios helped him to remove his tie and shirt.

Remedios began working on his wound, starting with that local anesthetic that she kept in her medical bag. While she worked, she spoke to him in a soft, reassuring voice.

"Lie down. Close your eyes and try to relax," she said.

Chito tried his best. He closed his eyes. He could feel her working on his wound.

"So, Chito, when was your last vacation?" Remedios ask.

He opened his eyes. Logan was watching, a slight smile on his face.

"Close your eyes and let me hear some slow, calm breathing," she said.

"Okay." He closed his eyes. He tried to calm his breathing. "My last vacation was about four years ago. It didn't last long. They called me back because there was a wave of break-ins on Fourth Avenue."

"So, if you were going on vacation now, where would you go and what would you do?" As she spoke to him, Remedios continued to work on his wound, cleaning it, and beginning the process of putting in stitches to hold the jagged tear together.

Chito took a deep breath. "I guess I'd go to the Yucatan. Maybe Cancun. No, not Cancun. Isla Mujeres. Yeah, that's where I'd go. I went there once when I was younger. It's a beautiful place."

"That's an island just off the coast of the Yucatan Peninsula?"

"That's right. Near Cancun." He opened his eyes.

"Close your eyes."

"Yes, ma'am." He closed his eyes.

"What would you do there on the island if you were on vacation?" she asked.

"Walk on the beach. Go swimming. Ride bicycles around the island." He sighed.

Logan spoke up now. "That sounds like a place that Zoey and Charlie and I would really like for a vacation." Logan was impressed with Remedios. She was obviously quite good at what she was doing as she treated Chito. Plus that, she was calm and comforting, and she was doing a great job of reassuring a reluctant patient. He wished he had an empty apartment for her. He would very much like to make her a part of the Casa Pacifica family.

The stitches were in place now. Remedios smeared some antibiotic cream over them, and put a bandage on top of the wound. "Chito, I'm going to give you an antibiotic injection now. We don't want an infection to get started."

"Okay."

"I'm also going to give you a second injection to help you sleep for a little while."

Chito opened his eyes. "Drugs? I don't want any drugs."

"This is a very mild sedative, just for a couple of hours of pain relief so you can rest. Later, you can go without any pain killers, and you can hurt as much as you want. For now, please trust me."

Chito sighed again. "Okay. I trust you."

Remedios gave him both injections. She turned to Logan. "You can go on home, if you wish. I'll sit with him for a while to make sure there's no drug reaction."

"I'm so glad you're here, Remedios. I wish I had a place open for you so you could live here," Logan said quietly.

Remedios smiled. "Not to worry. Everything will work out the way it's supposed to."

She settled into a chair near Chito. He was already drifting off.

"Okay. I'll be going. Thanks so much, Remedios."

She nodded. "My pleasure, Logan."

When Chito woke up, the sun was going down. He suddenly remembered what had happened. His arm hurt but not as bad as earlier. He remembered Remedios and how much she'd helped him, but she wasn't there anymore. She'd thrown a light-weight blanket over him before she left. He wanted to thank her. He hoped she would return.

Chito pulled himself up from the sofa and headed for the shower. He was careful to not get his bandage wet. Ten minutes later, he dressed himself in a clean shirt and pants and went into his kitchen looking for something to eat. He couldn't find anything. He heard a soft knock on his door so he went to open it.

Remedios was standing there smiling at him. "I'm here to check on you."

Chito returned her smile. "I'm doing great."

"Sit down and take your arm out of your sleeve so I can see."

Chito did as instructed. Remedios pulled back his bandage, looked closely, then reattached the bandage.

"Looks good," she said. "Do you need another injection for pain?"

"No, I need an injection for hunger. I'm starving."

Remedios stood up. "Okay, you're coming with me. I'll feed you."

Chito shook his head. "You don't have to do that."

"I'm hungry, too, and I think you'll be good company. But I warn you. The meal won't be anything gourmet."

Chito followed Remedios to Frida's apartment where she was staying. She sat him down at her kitchen table, and Chito looked around. He'd never been in Frida's apartment. He found it rather messy, like someone who never tidied up anything. It reminded him of his childhood home where his mother could never keep up with the chaos created by a large family. He could hear something being heated in a microwave.

"I know this place is really disorganized," Remedios said as she began frying tortillas. "But Frida told me to leave things alone," she continued. "She thinks if I organize this place then she won't be able to find anything."

Chito nodded. "Doesn't Frida have a cat?"

"Yes, the cat's name is Bonita. But she lives upstairs with Li most of the time."

"Prefers Chinese over Mexican?"

Remedios laughed. "Li is a way better cook than Frida. I think Li gives that cat some special treats, so Bonita eats better with Li. And Li's there a lot of the time. Frida is gone a lot so Bonita gets more attention with Li." She put some food bowls on the table. Chito recognized steaming frijoles, salsa, a dish of heated, fried ground beef, lettuce, and grated cheese. His stomach growled.

"Here's your plate and some silverware, and a glass of ice water. Like I said, nothing exciting."

"My favorites." He began eating enthusiastically. Remedios made a taco, but before she took her first bite, Chito was starting on his second.

He took a bite of the second taco, then paused. "I want to thank you for taking care of Isabel and me. Both of us. I really appreciate it."

Remedios smiled. "There's a price to pay for my care."

"Oh. I never thought of that. I can pay you. How much do you want?"

"No, silly. Not with money. I want information."

"Information? What kind of information?"

"I want to know you better, Chito Alvarez. Like how many times have you been shot?"

"Only three times, counting this wound today."

"*Only* three times!"

"Comes with the job. Yeah, my job is a cop's job, and sometimes we get shot. One time was serious, and I had to spend a couple of days in the hospital. That's why I don't ever want to go to the hospital. I don't like the hospital."

Remedios nodded. "Why did you become a cop?"

Chito frowned. He started eating a third taco.

Remedios chuckled. "Remember? You owe me."

He looked at her, still frowning. Then he relaxed and smiled. "Okay. Okay."

"So?" she asked. "Why did you become a cop?"

Chito took a long drink of ice water. "Well, Miss Davila. I graduated from the university with a degree in business administration. I did that to make my mother happy because she wanted me to be able to get a job and pay off my student loans."

"What did you really want to study?"

"I didn't know. I was really young."

"Did you find a job?"

"Yes, in a very large real estate company. I quit after six months. The job was boring, and I had to stay indoors in an office all day." He looked at the food on the table. "Can I have another taco?"

"You can have as many as you want. But why did you become a cop?"

"A friend of mine told me about openings at the Tuscon Police Department. I applied to TPD and was accepted. I liked the idea of not being stuck in an office all day, and I figured there would be some excitement if I worked there. I started as a patrolman and eventually moved up to detective."

Remedios laughed. "Yes, I guess getting shot can be viewed as exciting."

Chito started on his fourth taco. "These are terrific. You're a very good cook."

She laughed again. "You're not very picky."

"I don't really like to cook. And these are definitely delicious."

"Why did you divorce Isabel's mother?"

Why was she asking these questions? Chito asked himself. And why the hell was he answering her?

"We started dating in high school. She got pregnant. So we got married. Isabel was born when I was in college, and also I was working full time. We drifted apart. My wife didn't like it that I was gone all the time. Isabel was still a baby when we split up."

"Do you have a woman in your life now?"

Chito choked. "A woman?"

"Yes. Like a *novia*, a sweetheart, a girlfriend, a lover?"

Chito looked down. "No." How embarrassing. "I've had girlfriends since I got divorced, but they all got fed up with me. I work all the time, and sometimes, I get shot. So, no, there's no woman in my life now, and there hasn't been for a while."

"Ah, so that's what's wrong with you."

"Wrong with me? There's nothing wrong with me."

"My intuition about you is that you are a kind and loving man who would benefit from a personal relationship. You need that to be happy. You deserve to be happy."

Chito didn't know what to say to that.

"You're turning red, Chito Alvarez." She was smiling at him.

He started another taco, then put it down on his plate. Enough of all this being embarrassed stuff, he said to himself. He could be blunt, too. Chito looked at Remedios directly. "So, do you have a prescription to fix my problem?"

She grinned. "Perhaps I do. We'll see."

That dimple again. Chito noticed again that she was very pretty.

They were interrupted by a knock at her door. Remedios went to the door and found Li and Xochi standing there. Xochi's face was red and her eyes were full of tears, and Li had a very serious look on his face.

"Is Detective Alvarez here? Chito, I mean." Li asked.

"Yes, come in."

Chito was on his feet now. "What's going on?"

"We told you about our new gallery and music venue at the potluck," Li said. "When we returned home this afternoon after my food truck gig, we walked to the gallery and found that it had been vandalized."

"How bad is it?" Chito asked. "Any theft? I mean theft of art, equipment, anything?"

Xochi shook her head. "The art wasn't up on the wall yet. It was all together in the backroom in my studio. The paintings weren't touched. And my equipment and supplies seem to be okay."

"Yeah," Li added. "The damage is in the main front room where the gallery and music events will be. The walls have spray-painted graffiti all over them, and one wall has a hole punched in the sheet rock. The front window has a big crack in the glass, and the front door window glass was totally broken. I think that's how they got in – by breaking the front door glass."

"Does the graffiti say anything threatening?"

"No. It's just random marks in red paint. No words."

"Did you call TPD?"

Li nodded. "Yes, and a couple of cops came by. They said that a detective would come in the morning to ask us some questions and try to figure out who did this."

"I can be that detective. I'm supposed to be taking the week off, but this is a special case. I'll call my boss and get the go-ahead. Can we start fairly early? Let's meet at the gallery at nine in the morning?"

"Yes, thank you, Chito," Li said. Xochi added her thanks, too. She stepped forward and reached up to kiss Chito on his cheek.

Chito glanced over at Remedios. She was smiling.

Li and Xochi left, and Chito turned to Remedios. "I guess I should get some rest. But I could do the dishes first."

"Very good idea to get some rest. So go home now and get a good night's sleep. That's my wellness prescription for you, Chito. For now, anyway. And I'll do the dishes." Remedios reached up and kissed Chito on the cheek just as Xochi had done.

Chito went to his apartment and to his bed feeling confused about all the strange things that had happened that day, chief among them his interactions with Remedios. He didn't know what to think about her. Why was she asking so many questions? And why was he answering her? He must really trust her. Yeah, he trusted her. He didn't know why, but he trusted her. Chito closed his eyes. He fell asleep almost immediately.

3 THE INVESTIGATION BEGINS

Logan woke up early. He stayed very still lying next to Zoey who was curled up against him. He listened to her breathing. Soft, slow, peaceful. She was breathing for three: herself and those two little creatures growing inside her. He smiled, remembering how Zoey had told everyone that he'd "done a number" on her. His part in creating these new humans was easy and oh-so-pleasurable. But, for Zoey, it wouldn't be so pleasurable at every step in her nine month journey, which would end in the epic event of the twins' entry into the world. Logan was determined to do everything in his power to make her safe and happy. His son Charlie came into mind. Logan had been telling Charlie what to expect about new babies in the house. Charlie was beside himself with excitement. "I'm going to be a big brother!" he said repeatedly.

Easing himself away from Zoey, Logan slipped on some jeans and a t-shirt and went into the kitchen to start a pot of coffee. As he sipped his first cup, he sat quietly on his sofa watching the street below him in the Iron Horse neighborhood. He thought about his former student Darren, and the pain the young man was experiencing at the loss of his beloved girlfriend. Logan hoped someone friendly came to get Darren out of jail

and take him home. He hoped that Darren would figure out a way to cope with his loss because Logan knew
what that was like. Zoey came to mind, and he smiled.
Then the events of yesterday afternoon came to mind.
Watching Remedios Davila take care of Chito Alvarez
and his bullet wound gave Logan a great deal of solace.
An excellent police detective to protect them all, and an
excellent nurse practitioner to care for them if anyone
were hurt. And an excellent chef and an excellent artist.
Two excellent artists and an excellent veterinarian, too.
Who could ask for better Casa Pacifica tenants? And
friends.

Logan heard Charlie beginning to stir. He glanced at
the clock. Time to get up and start breakfast for his family.

* * *

Logan had just said goodbye to Zoey and Charlie when
he received a text. He read a brief message from Chito
saying that he was meeting Xochi and Li at their gallery
because the gallery had been vandalized, and would Logan like to come, too? 'Sure,' he responded. Fifteen minutes later, he joined Chito, and they began their blocks-
long walk to the Iron Horse businesses not too far from
Fourth Avenue.

"What's this about?" Logan asked Chito as they
walked west. "I thought you were taking the week off."

"Yeah, my chief told me that I needed to chill a bit.
But I texted him this morning, and he gave me the go-
ahead to work on this case. This situation is different.
I mean," he shrugged his shoulders, "Xochi and Li are
Casa Pacifica residents. We have to take care of our own,
right?"

"I'm really glad you think that way." Logan nodded.

Yeah, but it's more complicated than that, Chito said to himself. The real problem was that he didn't know what to do with himself when he wasn't working.

"By the way, thanks for helping me with that former student of yours. The way he was waving that gun around meant it could have gone off, and someone could have been badly hurt or worse," Chito said.

Logan nodded. "Thank you for being patient and giving me a chance to talk to him."

"If you don't mind saying more, what's this about someone named Caroline? She was your wife?"

"Yes, my first wife. She's Charlie's mother. Or was. We were sitting outside drinking coffee one morning when she suddenly touched her head and sort of sputtered 'It really hurts.' Then she passed out. I called for an ambulance, and they took her off to the hospital. Two hours later she was dead. She had a brain aneurysm, and she never woke up. It was a big shock, and it took me a while to get back on my feet. Charlie was only two at the time."

"So this was about three years ago? That's so sad." Chito paused. "I guess Zoey helped you to get back on your feet."

"Almost four years ago now," Logan answered. "Yes, Zoey changed everything for the better. She fell in love with Charlie, and then she fell in love with me. I think I loved her from the moment I first saw her, although it took me a while to figure that out. I can be clueless when it comes to women."

"I get that. I have the same problem."

"Also. you should know that Zoey was married before me. She had a very sick kid, sick from cystic fibrosis, who died when he was three. Her husband, the father of the sick boy, just took off, abandoning them both. Didn't want to be bothered."

33

"Some dudes are real dickheads."

Logan nodded. "Yeah. Look, we're almost here."

Ahead of them, they could see the *Clouds* sign on display hanging above the gallery's entrance door. As they neared, they could see that the front door had a plywood cover where glass had been. Two workmen were replacing the larger glass window which was cracked.

They entered the gallery. Xochi and Li were preparing to paint two different walls with an off-white paint. It looked to Chito that they might have to do a second coat to completely cover the graffiti on the two major walls. Lots of graffiti.

"Hey!" Xochi called out. "You're here!"

"Yeah, thanks for coming," Li added. "You, too, Logan."

"Can you take a break and answer a few questions for me?" Chito asked.

"Sure. Let's come into the back room. I'm already calling it my studio." Xochi pulled up two chairs, and Li brought two more.

Chito looked around. The room did indeed look like a studio. There were shelves filled with art supplies, and there was a big table in the middle of the room. He could also see a desk with a computer in one corner. High, narrow windows around the studio brought in some light, the skylights brought in even more.

"Okay. First, you said that the front door glass had been smashed? I see plywood there now." Chito gestured to the door.

"Yes," Li responded. "We couldn't very well leave it broken overnight. Anyone could walk in. So we called one of the guys who has been working on this place. He came in late and put plywood on the door. He'll replace the glass later after he and the other guy finish replacing the cracked big window."

"Tell me about the police officers who came yesterday," Chito continued.

"There were two of them," Xochi said. "They asked questions, took some photos, and one of them dusted the front door knob and part of the broken glass."

Li nodded in agreement. "They said they were looking for fingerprints. But they didn't find anything. No prints, I mean. It looks like the vandal had gloves on, or something. I don't know."

Chito nodded. "Anything else?"

Li continued. "They asked if anyone had been bothering us. Any notes or emails or phone calls threatening us. But we've haven't had anything like that. The neighbors seem happy that we've moved in and are opening up."

"Yeah, the woman next door has a yoga studio. She said she thinks we'll bring more customers to her so she's happy," Xochi said. "Her name is Melinda. She said an art gallery was a classy addition to the neighborhood."

"Another dude came in and asked about the music venues. He said he has a small jazz group. He gave me a card." Li stood up and walked to the desk, retrieved the card, and brought it to Chito. The card said: "Sonora Jazz Group." The photo on the front showed a pianist, bass player, and guitarist. There was a website URL and three names on the back. "But I think he was looking for a gig for his group," Li said. "He had no reason to vandalize this place."

Chito nodded. "Anyone else?"

"One day, when Li wasn't here because he was doing his food truck gig, a man came in," Xochi said. "He asked me what kind of business we were opening. I introduced myself and told him our plans. The gallery will be open Thursday through Saturday, and we'll have music events, maybe once a month, on Saturday evenings. Later we'll up the music to weekly. I'm setting aside the other days, Sunday through Wednesday, for me to teach my classes."

"Did he seem to have anything in mind? Like show his art or play music or something?"

"The dude said his name was Jack Something. He told me that he helps promote businesses and maybe he could help me. I just shrugged my shoulders and said we weren't ready for that yet. I told him that we didn't even have an opening date set yet. We do now, but not at that time. Then Li came in, and he pretty much repeated for Li what he'd said to me."

Li nodded. "He was only here for a few minutes."

"When was this?" Chito asked.

"About ten days ago or even two weeks ago," Xochi answered. "We were still moving my art and supplies into the studio. We hadn't even started painting the gallery walls yet."

"Describe him," Chito said.

"Not very tall, a little plump, middle-aged, going bald. He was grinning the whole time."

"Anyone else?"

"There have been numerous people who have stuck their heads in the door and waved to us and who have given us the thumbs-up sign," Li added. "But not anyone memorable."

"Do you have a surveillance camera?" Chito asked.

"No," Li answered. He glanced over at Xochi. "Maybe we should think about getting one."

"Oh, I forgot. Jack gave me his card." Xochi jumped up and went to the desk with the computer. She opened a drawer, retrieved the card and gave it to Chito.

Chito looked at the card and read aloud, "Jack Davis. Advertising and Promotions Consultant." There was an email address and phone number, but no website. The front of the card had a drawing of a large apartment complex. It looked familiar to Chito. But then, those large complexes always seemed to look the same to him. He put the card in his breast pocket.

"Okay. I'll look into this." Chito looked at Xochi and Li both. "How about something personal? Xochi, your family in Mexico? Has anyone been harassing you?"

"No, I don't hear much from them at all, especially since my half-brother was killed in that shootout. I'm no longer useful to them. Seems to me that they just wrote me off."

"How about you, Li? Any problem with your food truck?"

"No. On the contrary, I'm getting more and more business. I recently hired someone to work part time. Xochi's been helping me, but she can't be there every day."

Xochi grinned. "Li is an excellent cook. The food is great, and the menu has a lot of new Chinese dishes that most of us have never tasted. And we love it! Don't forget that the cook is really handsome."

Chito smiled. He turned to Li. "Okay. How about the restaurant where you used to work? I understand that you won several chef awards when you were working there. I bet they didn't like it that you quit."

Li nodded. "You're right about that. They definitely weren't happy."

"Have you heard from anyone there?"

"I got several email and phone messages from the manager, but I never responded. One of the workers told me that he was fired eventually. Then I got a call from the owner of the restaurant. I answered that call. We talked briefly, and he offered me a big pay raise plus a cut of the profits. I told him that I was much happier doing what I do now. So I said no. He got the message because he hasn't contacted me again. One day, when I was cooking at my food truck, three kitchen workers that I used to work with at the restaurant showed up. They asked if there was any chance I might open my own restaurant. They said they'd rather work for me."

"Your response?"

"I told them pretty much what I'm telling everyone. I'm happy now. I don't want to be trapped working in a restaurant every evening. I control my own hours and days with the food truck gig. And now I have a chance to play music. Best of all, I get to spend more time with Xochi. So far, I'm managing to support myself, so money isn't an issue."

Chito nodded. He understood completely. Being able to do work you love on your own terms, to have a personal interest like music, and best of all, to be with your lover and best friend, seemed to Chito like a really good life.

"Please write down the name of the restaurant where you worked, the owner's name, and the name of the manager that gave you so much grief."

Li went to the desk, found a slip of paper, and wrote the information that Chito requested.

Chito looked at Logan who had been quiet the entire time. "Anything you want to ask, or say?"

"Looks like you've covered everything, Detective. I'm going home now so you can do your investigation in the neighborhood without having to deal with me following you around." Logan looked at Xochi. "But what about the opening you told us about at the potluck? Has that been delayed?"

"No!" Xochi grinned. "We're going ahead."

Li nodded. "I'm cutting back on my food truck gig this week. We can get the walls painted by the end of today. The windows will be fixed by this evening, too. We think we can start hanging artwork tomorrow."

"Yeah, the paint dries fast. Meanwhile, I've been putting announcements out on social media about the opening. I've designed a poster that's at the printer now. We'll put up posters, too."

"A lot of work," Chito said.

"Yes, but fun," Xochi assured him.

"I'm going to be making refreshments for the opening, too," Li added.

"Sounds good. Okay. That's enough for now. Thanks," Chito said. He and Logan stood up and said their good-byes.

"See you back at home," Logan said. "I have papers to grade."

Chito nodded. "Let me know if you think of anything relevant."

"You asked good questions," Logan said. "I think you'll figure this out." He reached out and shook Chito's hand. "See you later." He turned and began the walk back to Casa Pacifica Apartments.

Chito looked around. He was on one of the streets in the far west of the Iron Horse neighborhood, very close to the north-south Fourth Avenue, which was crowded with multiple business, shops, restaurants, and bars. He decided to go to the Fourth Avenue later and, instead, now he would check out locations near the new Clouds gallery to see if he could find any evidence of break-ins, vandalism, or other crimes.

He stepped out of Clouds gallery and looked around. He could see a couple of large high-rise apartment buildings south of the street where he was standing. One was about a half a block behind Clouds gallery, and the other was in the next block to the east. He looked up and down the Clouds gallery street. There were residential houses in this block, mainly on the side of the street opposite the gallery. Based on signs he could see, some of the homes had been turned into offices for small businesses. There was a lawyer's office in one house, and a tattoo salon in another. On the side of the street where he was standing, he could see the yoga studio that Xochi had mentioned. To the west of the yoga studio was the neighborhood grocery store, which most residents referred to as "our market." To the east, there was a bicycle repair shop, a small coffee shop, an accounting firm, and beyond that, more homes, then a small apartment complex. Across the street, he could see a homeless man sitting on the sidewalk, a can for collecting donations in front of him. The man had a sign on cardboard that said, "Help. Homeless. Hungry."

Chito went to the yoga studio first. He walked in the front door and found a young woman sitting behind a desk. She smiled and said, "Are you here for our beginner's yoga class? It starts in half an hour. Do you have any comfortable clothes to wear? That suit and tie makes you really handsome, but it's not all that comfortable for yoga."

Chito retrieved his detective identification card from his front pocket. "I'm a Tucson Police Department detective. My name is Detective Alvarez, and I'm investigating the break-in and vandalism next door. Do you have time to answer a few questions?"

The young woman frowned. "Sure. I'm Melinda. I can't tell you how pissed off I am that those buttheads vandalized the new place. To have an art gallery, an art studio, and a place for musicians to share their music is the best. Wow! I couldn't ask for anything better. It will be great for me to visit, and also, I'm pretty sure it will bring me more business."

"So do you know who the 'buttheads" are, by any chance?"

"No, I didn't see them."

"Were you here yesterday evening? And what time does your studio close in the evening?"

"The last class is over at eight p.m. Usually everyone is gone by eight thirty. I lock up and leave. When I left, the gallery looked normal. The front door hadn't been broken into. The big glass window hadn't been cracked."

"Do you have a surveillance camera?"

She shook her head no.

"Has anyone come here and tried to intimidate or harass you in anyway?"

"No. My yoga customers are usually the only visitors. The only one who harasses me is my ex-boyfriend." A sultry look appeared on Melinda's face. "Do you have a girlfriend, Detective?"

Chito shook his head. "Not now. I'm too busy."

"You need to relax. How about if you come in for a free yoga class. Or a massage." She smiled and wiggled her eyebrows.

Good grief, Chito said to himself silently. "I'm sorry, Melinda, but I am seriously busy. No time for yoga or a massage."

"Too bad." Her lips went into a pout.

He reached into his pocket and retrieved his business card. "If anyone approaches you and demands anything of you, here's my card. You can contact me at my office." Chito handed her his card.

Melinda looked at it and smiled at him.

Uh oh, he thought to himself. This world-class flirt might start calling him for no good reason. "Business only," he said.

Melinda made a face.

Chito left quickly and went into the market next door. He asked a couple of the store clerks if they'd seen anything. Next he spoke with the manager.

"We close at ten p.m.," the manager told him. "Usually our street is pretty quiet by then. The noise at that time of night comes from the clubs over on Fourth Avenue."

"Do you have a surveillance camera?"

"We do, but it's not working now," the manager said. "That's on my list of things to get fixed." He frowned.

The fact that the break-in occurred after the market closed told Chito that the break-in must have occurred fairly late at night, definitely well after ten p.m. He gave the manager his card and asked for a call if the manager learned anything about the break-in or other problems in the area. Next, he systematically visited the lawyer's office, the accountant's, the bike shop, and the tattoo parlor. He bought a cup of coffee at the coffee shop. Everywhere he went, he asked the same questions. No one had anything useful to say. No one had seen anything. Several places had surveillance cameras, but they were all directed at the house's or the shop's front entrance. The entrance to Clouds gallery was not being picked up by any of the surveillance cameras.

He decided to try the homeless man. Chito went into the market and purchased a chicken and cheese sandwich and a big cup of iced tea. He figured it was better to give this guy food to eat rather than money to spend on drugs. He crossed the street, knelt down next to the man and handed him the food and drink.

"Thanks, Officer." He took the sandwich and began to unwrap it.

Chito's eyebrows went up. "How did you know I'm a cop?"

The man smiled. "I have experience with cops."

Chito noticed that he was maybe fifty something years old, with a sun-browned, wrinkled face and an untrimmed beard.

"I'm Detective Alvarez. What's your name?"

"Alexander."

"I'm investigating the vandalism that occurred across the street. Did you see or hear anything?"

"Yeah. I saw 'em do it."

"You saw the vandals?" Chito was surprised.

"At night, I sleep on my big pillow behind that creosote bush over there." He gestured to a house a couple of doors down. As mentioned, there was a large creosote bush in the front yard next to the sidewalk. "They woke me up when they smashed the glass."

"How many of them were there?"

"Only two of them. Two big guys. The kind of guys I avoid because they like to beat up on people like me."

"What did you see them do?"

"They both had hammers and went for the glass first. That made it possible for them to get into the gallery. They turned on flashlights, and I could see them decorating the walls of the gallery with spray paint. The whole thing took maybe five or ten minutes max. Then they came out and ran toward Fourth Avenue."

"Did you recognize either of them?"

"They were dressed in dark clothes. They had on hoodies so it wasn't easy to see their faces. But one of them turned my way, and the street light caught him for a moment. I'd say he looked familiar to me, but I don't know who he was or where I'd seen him."

"If you see him again, do you think you could identify him?"

Alexander shrugged his shoulders. "I'm not sure."

Chito handed him his card. "Call me if you have more information."

Alexander nodded. "Thanks for the sandwich and the tea."

"No problem." Chito stood up. He glanced at his watch. Early afternoon now, and he realized his stomach was growling. He headed home to Casa Pacifica Apartments, thinking about ordering some take-out food to be delivered to his place. He'd have a really good late lunch.

4 A VISIT, A LETTER

Logan walked home quickly, vowing to himself to start exercising more regularly. He'd become more disciplined about exercise in recent months, but he felt it wasn't enough. He needed to be strong and healthy so he could take care of his growing family. Three kids! Oh, my god. He would also have to learn to be more patient. Three kids were going to take a lot of patience.

He arrived at his office by late morning, only to find that there was a pile of student papers waiting for him in his inbox. He decided to take them home and grade them there. He checked emails for anything important and found a message from Darren, the young man who had been waving that gun around on Sunday morning.

The message read: "Dear Mr. Reid, Thank you very much for helping me the other day. I drank way too much. Tequila and bourbon don't really mix well. And then I took that pill that my friend said would make me feel better. It didn't make feel better. I kinda lost my mind. You helped me get back on track. So I got rid of the gun. I got rid of the booze. I got rid of the pills, and I got rid of the 'friend' who gave me the pill. I think I'll study philosophy more and learn how to stop worrying and be happy, Your student, Darren."

Logan sat back in his chair and smiled. Sometimes he felt overwhelmed. He wasn't sure himself exactly how to stop worrying and be happy. But in this case, he'd done the right thing. He clicked on Reply.

"Thanks for the message, Darren. Excellent idea to study philosophy. Wikipedia has a good article titled 'Philosophy of Happiness,' with a list of philosophers who have written about what happiness is and how to achieve it. As for me, my family makes me happy. You know I have a son from my first marriage. You met my first wife Carolyn who died suddenly. My son's name is Charlie. He's very happy because Zoey, my wife, is pregnant with twins. Charlie has announced to the world about ten million times that he's going to be a big brother. So I'm not worrying. Well, I still worry some, for sure, but I am happy now. You'll get there. Never give up. Logan Reid."

Immediately after clicking on Send, Logan heard a soft knock at his door.

"Come in," he called out.

The door opened, and a young woman appeared. She was smiling. "Hi, Mr. Reid."

Logan's eyebrows went up. Who was she? Had to be a former student. Name? He couldn't remember.

"I bet you don't remember me. I'm Alyssa Fredericks, now Alyssa Johnson. I got married and took my husband's name. I was in your Intro to Philosophy class when I was a student at the University of Arizona."

"Oh, yeah. I remember you." Sort of remember, Logan said to himself. "How are you?"

"I'm good."

"Come in and sit down." He had this vague memory of her as a young student, probably just a freshman or sophomore, always dressed in blue jeans and a flannel shirt, very quiet, who rarely said anything in class. She looked quite different now, dressed in a suit and low heels.

"What brings you to Pima Community College? Are you still a student at the UofA?"

"No. I'm not a student anywhere. I dropped out when I got married nearly a year ago. Actually I've been thinking about enrolling here. I thought maybe it wouldn't be so stressful."

"Stressful? So you found the University of Arizona stressful?"

"Yes. I'm kind of shy and the other students in my classes there seemed to know everything already. Some of the professors were pretty harsh. I was scared to talk."

Logan's eyebrows went up. "I'm sorry to hear that. Was my class like that for you?"

"No. Well, maybe sometimes. But most of the time, your classes were more relaxed."

"That's good to know. Do you know what you want to study?"

"I'm thinking about business, and specifically, marketing."

"You're interested in marketing?" He tried to smile. For Logan, he'd rather do anything than attempt to sell something.

"This is probably going to sound weird. I married a man who is older than me. I'm twenty-one now. He's thirty-seven. He's very successful, he has several businesses, and he's about to open another one."

"What kind of business is he in?"

"Different things. Real estate, mainly. He buys and sells properties, he has a team to manage them, and he also appraises properties. He even has a B&B for out-of-town visitors, and he owns a couple of restaurant bars."

Busy man, Logan thought.

Alyssa continued, "I was thinking that if I knew more about marketing, maybe I could help him with his business. Maybe he'd have more free time, too. He's building

47

a new apartment complex now, and he'll be renting the apartments when it's done. I don't want him to get bored with me. I'd like to help him."

Two different problems, Logan thought.

"I mean, if he needs help getting attention for the new business that he's working on, I'd like to help him. What do you think would be the best way to do marketing?"

"Gosh, Alyssa. I don't know much about that kind of thing. Social media, maybe? Or advertising?" He shook his head.

"That makes sense," she said.

"Where is the new apartment building?"

"It's just east of Fourth Avenue, a couple of blocks near the south end of Fourth, I think. I haven't actually been there."

Logan's eyebrows went up. Her description put the apartment building in the Iron Horse neighborhood.

"You may think it's presumptuous of me, but I'd like to make a suggestion. Okay?" Logan asked.

"Please do. I've always thought of you as one of the nice guys."

"Think about seeing a counselor, and talk to her or him about your feelings of being stressed and about fear that your husband might get bored with you. It's possible that you could learn how to handle stress better. And you might discover that you are not perceiving your husband's behavior and his motivations correctly."

"Oh." She had a surprised look on her face. "So maybe I don't have to worry about him getting bored?"

"A counselor could help you figure that out."

She nodded. "Okay. I get what you're saying."

"And then, based on what you have come to understand about your marriage, you could decide if you really and truly are interested in marketing, and if you want to go ahead with studying it."

Alyssa stood up. "I knew I could count on you, Mr. Reid. You've given me a lot to think about. You've been very helpful."

Logan nodded. "I wish I could be of more help. A counselor would be your best bet to get some good help."

She was moving toward the door now. "Bye, Mr. Reid. Thanks so much."

"Take care of yourself, Alyssa."

Logan sat and thought for a while. He wondered why Alyssa was so shy and, apparently, very unsure of herself. Had she been born that way or had she been treated harshly as a child and lost all her self-confidence? Who knew? He couldn't help but wonder why a thirty-seven-year-old man would marry someone so shy and so young. Alyssa was pretty. Maybe it was all about sex, and maybe her husband wanted to feel better about himself as a virile man if he could attract a younger woman. Or maybe he wanted her to be one of those women he showed off to bring in more business. Charlie popped into his head. Logan could say for sure that Charlie didn't have that insecurity problem. Charlie had a lot of self-confidence, and he liked to talk a lot and give everyone his opinion about everything under the sun. No, he didn't have Alyssa's problem. Charlie will be a good big brother, Logan decided.

Enough of this. Logan piled the students' papers into his briefcase and headed home. He wanted to arrive before Zoey so he could make her some lunch. And he did just that.

After lunch, they sat together on their sofa and observed the world going by through their big front window. After some moments of quiet, Zoey spoke first.

"Logan, do you know what happened to that young man who was waving the gun around Sunday morning? I was watching from the window. It was scary."

"Yeah, I knew him because he'd been one of my students. I was glad that Chito didn't let the situation get out of hand. It would have been awful if Darren had been shot."

"Or you or Chito," Zoey added.

"Yes, that would have been bad, too. When I went to my office, I found an email he'd sent me. His name is Darren. He's a smart kid, and he's handling this well. He said in his email that there would be no more guns, no more booze, and no more drugs. He said he's going to study philosophy. I approve."

She chuckled. "Of course you do. The world needs more philosophers."

"I told him about the Philosophy of Happiness. I think he'll look up the links I sent." Logan paused. "I had another former student come in, too." Logan proceeded to tell Zoey about Alyssa Johnson and what she'd talked about.

"That's two different issues," Zoey said. "Her lack of self-confidence is one problem, the biggest problem. And the choice to be a marketer in the hopes that her husband will continue to care about her and not be bored by her is another problem, although these problems are linked."

"That's what I thought. Do you think I gave her good advice to go into counseling? I mean, I was being kind of presumptuous."

"Your advice is very good. She needs a trained person to help her begin to understand her own responses, and to understand her motivations. She needs counseling. And, for the record, well-liked teachers often get asked for advice from students and former students. You responded perfectly."

"I bet you get asked for advice a lot."

Zoey smiled. "Actually, I do. Yesterday, I was asked by one of my students, a girl, on how to prevent pregnancy."

"Could that kind of information going to a minor get you in trouble?"

"If I just told her about different forms of birth control, yes, I could get in trouble if her parents found out. But her question gave me an opportunity to get her to step back and take a bigger look at her herself and the situation, to ask herself if she was really ready for that kind of relationship, and to ask herself if she was being pressured to have sex. Things like that. I gave her some links to read about various birth control methods. But it was pretty clear from her reaction that she realized she had a lot to think about, especially when I asked her if she was being pressured by the boy."

Logan kissed her. "She's lucky that you are her teacher."

"I'm lucky that you love me."

"Anything else going on with my favorite teacher?"

"Students have been coming by to say goodbye, to wish me luck, and several have given me going-away gifts."

"Gifts? Like what?"

"Books, mostly about birds, but one is about twins, their genetics, growth patterns, all sorts of very interesting things about twins. And I was given a plant in a pot which I'll bring home soon. An art student gave me a small watercolor painting, and one of the students who makes jewelry gave me a pair of earrings that she'd made. Also I received a key chain with a thank you amulet."

"You deserve everything good that comes to you," Logan said. He put his arm around her shoulders. Zoey leaned against him. They were quiet for several minutes, then Zoey spoke again.

"Logan, there's something else. Maybe you can help me. I received a letter from the law firm that I hired several years ago to help me get a divorce from my first husband, the father of my little boy Josh. It's a certified letter. I had to sign for it."

Logan could hear the pain in her voice. Her son had died at the age of three from an incurable disease.

"How can I help you?" he asked.

"I don't want to open the letter. I don't know what it's about, and just looking at it makes me anxious. It brings back the trauma of my son's death. And I told you about how my ex, Josh's father, just walked out on us. I had to deal with Josh's death and the divorce and everything by myself."

"Want me to open it for you? I'll see what they want. If there's a problem, I'll do my best to deal with it for you."

Zoey lifted her head and looked at Logan. He could see tears in her eyes.

"Oh, my love. That would be so helpful. Yes, please. You read it. I knew I could count on you."

"No worries. Just leave the letter on my desk, and I'll take care of it."

Zoey snuggled up against him and whispered, "I'm the luckiest woman in the world."

After more time spent snuggling, a movement outside the window caught Logan's attention.

"Look, there's Chito. I want to ask him what happened after I left him this morning. Back in a minute." He jumped up and went to the door, opening it just as Chito entered the apartment building.

"Hey, Chito. Did you learn anything useful this morning?"

Chito nodded. "A little bit. Most of the people I interviewed knew nothing. There were a lot of surveillance cameras on the street, but they were all turned the wrong way or didn't work at all. Finally, I asked a homeless man. Turns out he'd seen everything. He said there were two men in hoodies who broke into the gallery late at night.

He saw them using flashlights when they were doing all that graffiti damage. They went straight to the gallery, did their dirty work really quickly, and made no attempt to break in anywhere else on the street."

"Sounds like the gallery was targeted. Not a couple of drunks raising hell."

"That's right. It took place late at night, and the break-in was likely planned in advance. The man I talked to said that one of the perps looked familiar, but he wasn't sure if he could identify him again."

"So this sounds like there's someone who wants to put Xochi and Li out of business before they even get started," Logan said.

Chito nodded. "My job is to figure who it is exactly that wants them out of business and why. And stop them. That's what I'll be working on this next."

"Okay. If there's anyway I can help, let me know," Logan said.

"I will. I'm going to go call my chief now."

Logan returned to his apartment and Zoey. He waited until Zoey went to their bedroom for a nap. As she grew in size carrying the twins, she often took afternoon naps. He shook his head. The idea of having a human being, or two human beings, growing inside of you was really hard for him to imagine. Sure. We all get here that way, he told himself. But he just couldn't imagine what it must feel like to have those little creatures moving around and kicking you from the inside. Weird. And wonderful, too. He sighed. He decided that he was glad he was a man.

Logan heard a noise outside and realized that it was time for Charlie to be coming home. He and another boy, an elementary student from the neighborhood, had been walking home together, accompanied by the other child's older sister who was in the eighth grade. Logan and Zoey decided together that Charlie was mature for his age and could be trusted to stay with his friend and his sister. And it was very convenient for Logan not to have to pick him up at school.

Logan jumped up, hurried to open the downstairs front door, and Charlie barged in. Logan waved goodbye to Charlie's friend and his sister.

"Try to be quiet, Charlie. Zoey's taking a nap."

"Can I go upstairs and see if Gwenny is home?"

"Sure." Charlie had plenty of friends, but Gwenny, the big greyhound dog, was his best friend. "Try to be quiet."

"I'll be quiet." Charlie dropped his backpack and ran up the stairs, not exactly quietly.

Logan heard Charlie knocking on Marc and Angela's door. Five minutes later, Charlie and Gwenny returned to Logan's apartment. The remainder of the afternoon and evening was taken up dealing with Charlie and Gwenny, then Zoey, then dinner preparation, then an evening of watching a movie together and reading a bedtime story. Logan forgot about the letter that Zoey had asked him to read until later. Zoey was already asleep and Logan was drifting off when he suddenly remembered the letter. He promised himself that he would read it tomorrow.

* * *

Not long after talking with Logan that afternoon, Chito entered his apartment and threw off his suit coat jacket. His gun in its holster went to its regular place on his desk. He reached for his phone to search for the website of Tumerico, his favorite Tucson restaurant. After a serious study of the menu, he decided on six dishes, way more than he could eat in one meal. The plan was to take a little from each dish to eat immediately, and freeze the rest for meals for the next couple of days. He called in his order, starting with the ropa vieja plate and the tamale plate. He added tacos and huevos rancheros. And mole. And burritos.

He sat down on his sofa and called the Chief of Police, Jake Sears.

"Chief, I went in and interviewed the two who are opening the gallery. They didn't have much useful to tell me. No one has been demanding anything of them, and they had no threats to report. Seems like everyone in the neighborhood is pleased to see them open their gallery and music venue. Workmen were replacing the broken glass, and the two who are opening the place, their names are Xochi and Li, were both repainting the vandalized walls. After talking to them, I went around to several businesses and homes, and I was able to establish that the break-in occurred late at night. No one had anything helpful to say until I talked to a homeless man who happened to be sleeping under a big bush across the street that night. He reported seeing two vandals breaking in and doing all the damage. He said he didn't know who they were, although he did think he may have seen one of the vandals before, but he wasn't sure. And he wasn't sure he could ID the guy if he saw him again."

"Okay. Looks like you're working on this case despite the fact you're supposed to be taking a leave. So I'll get one of my officers here to see if there's been any other similar cases of vandalism in the area recently. That would suggest this was more than just one random case of two vandals arbitrarily destroying property. But if there haven't been any other cases, that does seem strange that they chose only this one place, Clouds, and it hasn't even opened yet."

"I was thinking the same thing. I mean, if the perpetrators were just a couple of rowdies raising hell and destroying property, seems like more than one business would have been vandalized," Chito said.

"As for you, how is that gunshot wound?" the chief asked.

"Getting better. My nurse friend patched me up."

"Good. I suggest you just take a look around and see what you can see. Otherwise, take it easy."

"Will do. Talk to you later, Chief."

They said their goodbyes.

5 Lunch with Remedios

Chito happened to glance out his living room window just as Remedios passed by in the yard of Casa Pacifica. She was heading for the side entrance of the apartment building that led through the tiny kitchen and laundry room and directly to Frida's apartment where she was staying.

"Now or never," he muttered to himself as he jumped up and headed for his door. He opened it just as Remedios appeared at her door. She turned at the sound.

"Hi, Chito." She smiled.

"Uh...uh…" He stood there, his hands in his pockets. "Hi, Remedios. I was wondering if you'd like to eat lunch with me."

"Sure. You made some lunch?"

"Not exactly 'made.' I have an order coming from Tumerico."

Remedios chuckled. "Okay. Give me a few minutes. I had a job interview this morning so now I want to get out of these clothes and into something more comfortable."

"Fine. Come over when you're ready. I'll leave the door open for you."

Remedios knocked softly on his open door a few minutes later and called out, "Hello, it's me."

"Come on in." Chito looked at her. She had changed from a business suit into a full-length, patterned skirt, a white peasant blouse, and some bright blue socks and sandals. Her hair was down now, tousled dark curls on her shoulders. Lovely.

"The order will be here in a few minutes. Do you know about Tumerico?"

"No. I grew up in Tucson, but things have changed a lot since I lived here. There's a lot of new restaurants that I'm not familiar with."

"Tumerico is a vegan vegetarian restaurant that already has won a bunch of prizes. It's Mexican food."

Her eyebrows went up."You didn't strike me as a vegan or a vegetarian."

"I'm not. Truth is, I'll eat just about anything. I go for Tumerico's food because it tastes really good."

The doorbell to the front entrance of Casa Pacifica rang.

"I'll be right back," Chito said. He disappeared down the hall, pulling his wallet out of his pocket as he went. He returned quickly with a large bag in his hands. He opened it and began removing and placing the various containers on his kitchen table.

"Oh, so much food!" Remedios grinned. "It smells great."

"Here's the plan," Chito said, as he opened each container. "Take the dish you want and put it on your plate. Or take a portion of each dish. Whatever is left over will be my meals for tomorrow and the next day."

"Hmm...planning ahead. I guess you're not into cooking?"

Chito shook his head. "I have to cook when my daughter is here, but I just make simple stuff. Isabel is not picky, thank god. I don't really know any recipes or how to be a good cook so I just order out a lot. And sometimes my neighbor invites me over for some really great tacos."

Remedios nodded and smiled. "We'll do that again sometime soon." She began selecting portions from each container.

"Want something to drink? I don't have any beer or anything."

"Ice water would be good."

They sat in silence, eating, except for occasional expressions of delight at how delicious the food was. Finally, Remedios sat back and said, "I can't eat anymore. This was great. Thank you, Chito."

"Go sit on the sofa. I'll put all this away." Chito closed the containers and stuffed everything into the refrigerator. He joined her on the sofa. "So how did the job interview go?"

"Really well. I think they will offer me a position. I already have two job offers so I'll have to decide which to take. I thought maybe I'd be working in a hospital emergency room again, but the ER can get pretty hectic. So now I'm considering working in a specialists' medical clinic. I have an offer from a clinic devoted to pain management. The advantages of working in a clinic would be more regular hours and weekends off. That means I'd have some personal time and not be on call. On the other hand, the ER can be exciting and professionally challenging."

Chito nodded.

"That reminds me. Before I leave here today, I'd like to take a closer look at your arm," she said.

"You say that a lot. 'A closer look,' I mean." Chito smiled.

"I say that because it doesn't sound as serious and scary as demanding to examine your wound again."

"And you want your patients to feel safe?"

"I do. I do want everyone to feel safe with me."

"You made my daughter feel safe. I'm very grateful to you."

Remedios shrugged and smiled. A moment of silence followed.

"You want to know something, don't you, Detective Alvarez?"

Chito grinned. "Well, it's like this. When I ate tacos with you the other day, you asked me a lot of questions. Like you asked me about my family, my education, why I became a cop, and about my personal relationships."

Remedios smiled. "Did I offend you?"

"No. I'm just curious."

"You're curious about why I asked all those questions?"

"Yes, but even more, I'm curious about you. I'd like to ask you the same kind of questions and get some answers. I'd like to know you better."

"Well, you did feed me lunch, so I guess I owe you. Feel free to ask away. But I want to warn you that some of my answers may be unpleasant. I don't want to scare you."

"You can't scare me. You might disappoint me, though."

Her eyebrows went up. "Disappoint?"

"I'll let you know if that happens. So be as open and honest as I was with you. First, tell me about your family. I know you are Frida's half-sister."

"My mother and Frida's father split up when she was really little. My mother married another man who became my father. I had a pretty normal childhood until I was twelve years old." Remedios was staring at the wall now.

Chito noticed that tears had appeared in her eyes.

"My dad's brother, my uncle, raped me when I was twelve. He really hurt me. Actually, he raped me twice."

Chito gritted his teeth. "That's outrageous," he muttered.

"When my dad found out, he beat the shit out of my uncle and told him to get out of town and never come back. I never saw my uncle again. My parents decided to cover everything up so my uncle was never prosecuted. My parents encouraged me to pretend that the rapes had never happened."

Chito reached out and took her hand in his. "*Dios mío.* How did you ever survive that?"

"I had been a pretty cheerful kid up until then. But after that trauma, I turned into sort of a recluse. I stayed in my room, read books, never went out with friends, and certainly never went on dates with boys. Then, when I graduated from high school, I left home and moved into a Monastic Residence Program run by the Benedictine Sisters in New Jersey."

Chito couldn't think of anything she might have told him that could shock him more. Even more than a childhood rape, which happened way too often. "Oh, my god. You're a nun!" He felt a wave of disappointment wash over him.

Remedios looked at him and chuckled. "No. It was like I said, a residence program for young women. I lived there for two years. The nuns helped me tremendously to find myself again, to become centered, to heal from my trauma, and to figure out what I wanted to do with my life. At the end of two years, I had the option of becoming a nun, but I felt a calling to go into medicine. I didn't really want to return to Tucson at that time, so I applied and got a scholarship to go to school in Texas. That's how I ended up becoming a nurse practitioner. Until recently, I was working in a hospital ER in Kirby, which is part of the San Antonio metro area."

"What a story!" Chito shook his head. He was still holding her hand.

"I have this feeling that you're relieved that I'm not a nun." She smiled.

Chito nodded. "Very relieved. That would have disappointed me. Nuns are off limits as far as I'm concerned."

"No, I'm not off limits," she chuckled. "What else do you want to know?"

He was still for a moment. "This is sort of uncomfortable of me to ask, but you asked me about my personal relationships, so I'll ask you."

Remedios squeezed his hand. "You want to know if I've ever had sex with a man?"

He felt himself getting hot and embarrassed at the same time. "I don't think I was going to be quite that direct, but whatever. After what happened to you, I shouldn't even ask about personal relationships."

"The answer is yes. I was married for a while to a doctor. We were married for several years. We had a very good relationship, but then we began to drift apart. We eventually decided that each of us was going in a new direction so we divorced peacefully, without conflict. He ended up moving to Australia. Long story about how that came about. I consider him a very good friend, and we stay in touch. And yes, Jeff and I had sexual relations. We made love frequently, and we really enjoyed our physical intimacy. I miss having sex."

Chito groaned and then laughed. He was at a loss for words now.

"So after all that, I felt this calling to return to Tucson. My parents are aging, and I want to help take care of them. And I wanted to get to know my sister Frida better. Also I see opportunities to do volunteer medical work here, too. And I realized that my life's trauma and the pain had been dealt with, or dealt with as best I could. I decided that it was safe for me to return home. I love Tucson."

Chito sighed. "Well, for the record, that part about enjoying sex means that you didn't disappoint me, although I'll have to say that the thought of you being a nun scared the bejesus out of me for a minute there."

Remedios chuckled. "Okay. Now I'm going to tell you something that might scare you."

Chito looked at her and grinned. He never let go of her hand. "Let's hear it."

"I discovered when I was in the monastery that I am a little bit psychic."

Chito's eyebrows went up. "What do you mean?"

"I don't like to think of myself as psychic, so I probably shouldn't use that word, although that's the term the nuns used. Let's just say I'm very intuitive. I have immediate instinctive understandings about people sometimes. The nuns said my ability to perceive these things is a gift, a spiritual gift."

"Oh." Chito paused. "So is that what a cop might think of as a 'gut feeling'?"

"Yes, I suppose so. Does learning that about me scare you?"

"No. Not at all." He sat back, a thoughtful look on his face. "So what is your intuitive feeling about me?" He glanced sideways at her.

"The first time I saw you, I knew you were special. I had this feeling that I really need to get to know you because you may very well be the man for me."

His eyebrows went up again.

"Am I scaring you now?"

Chito grinned and shook his head no. "I'm not that easy to scare. And I'd say your intuition is convenient for me because I had the same kind of gut feeling about you, that you are special and I should pursue knowing you. Know you in every way, I mean, including intimately. What do you think we should do about this?"

"I think we should go slowly and really explore what's happening between us. We don't have to go really fast. We can go slowly and develop a rich and deep relationship. Then when the time is right, I want us to make love. I want you to wear your Minions pajamas so I can take them off of you." She giggled. "Those pajamas are very sexy."

Chito swallowed hard. "Oh, fuck it," he groaned. Reaching out, he pulled Remedios to him. His mouth connected with hers in a passionate kiss.

There was a sudden loud knock on his door. Chito could hear someone calling to him.

"Detective Alvarez? Chito? Are you at home?"

"Crap!" Chito groaned. "Always interruptions, and at the worst time."

Remedios laughed.

Chito went to the door and opened it. As he expected, Li and Xochi were standing there. Li's face was red, and Xochi's eyes were full of tears.

"Come on in," he said. "What's going on?" He noticed that Li had a large envelope in his hand.

When Li and Xochi saw Remedios, they said hello. She waved and smiled. "We've been stuffing ourselves with Tumerio dishes," she said.

Xochi nodded. "Good choice. Tumerico is terrific." She turned back to Li.

"We started getting mail delivery at the gallery today for the first time. This came in the mail." Li thrust the envelope into Chito's hand.

Chito opened the envelope and pulled out a paper covered with words scrawled in red ink. He read the words out loud. "Shut this shit hole down! Now! No opening on Saturday! Shut it down or you'll be sorry!"

Xochi sobbed.

Chito looked at Li. His face was red, and he looked furious. Chito nodded. "This is good."

"Good? What the hell?" Li said.

"Good because now we know that the vandalism wasn't random. You're being targeted. Now we need to figure out why you are a target and who is behind this."

Li nodded. "Okay. Okay. What should I do?"

Chito glanced at Xochi. "You take care of Xochi. We don't want the perps to find her alone and attack her." He noticed that Li's face was getting red again. "Meanwhile, I'm going to begin a serious investigation here. Dig deeper. You two watch your backs. I'll take the lead on this. I may have more questions for you later."

Li nodded. He turned to Xochi and put his arm around her shoulders. "Come on, sweetie. Let's go to our apartment now and get some rest. I'm going to take a break from the food truck for a while until we get this resolved. And you and I are sticking together, just like Chito said." He turned to Chito. "Thanks, bro."

"No problem. Stay in touch. Text me if anything comes up."

Xochi and Li left, and Chito heard them climbing the stairs. He turned to Remedios.

"What's a perp?" she asked.

"Short for 'perpetrator.' I have to call my chief now and update him." Chito called in and reported the latest news about the threatening note. In return, the chief told him that there had been no other similar incidents in the neighborhood recently. They agreed that the gallery had been targeted and the vandalism was not random. Chito signed off.

"Is there anything I can do to help?" Remedios asked.

Chito sat down next to her on the sofa. "Yeah, maybe. I think we should take a walk around that area near their gallery and see if there's anything unusual or out-of-place. I've questioned some people, and I identified myself as a cop. I may be recognized. But if I'm with you, it may deflect attention away from me. The fact that someone wants to make sure Clouds doesn't open suggests that the gallery is being perceived as some kind of threat, like maybe competition. We could pretend to be two lovers just enjoying being together while we look for anything odd."

"Pretending to be your lover will be good practice for the time when I actually become your lover." She smiled and batted her eyelashes.

Chito shook his head and grinned. "Don't tempt me. I might want to up the time line."

"For now, though, I want to take a closer look at your wound. So take your shirt off, Detective Alvarez."

"Yes, ma'am." He unbuttoned his shirt and pulled it off.

"Sit back and relax. I'm going to remove your bandage and see if there's any sign of infection."

Chito did as instructed. He noticed as she came closer that Remedios smelled really good.

"Looks good, Chito. No sign of infection. We'll leave things the way they are, and I'll check you again tomorrow."

"Can you take the stitches out?"

"Yes, of course, but not for several days. We'll see what the wound looks like as time passes."

She reattached the bandage, then she opened her palm and began stroking his chest with her fingertips. She leaned forward and kissed him on his neck and cheek.

Chito groaned. "You better stop, or our relationship won't be developing slowly. It will go warp speed ahead instead."

"Yes, sir." She pulled back. "Okay. Let's go take that walk you talked about."

"I need to get out of this suit. Maybe some jeans and a sweatshirt or something will make me look like an ordinary guy, not a cop snooping around. I have a little pork pie hat, too. I suggest you go to your apartment and get a sweater or jacket. When the sun goes down, it will get chilly."

"You could keep me warm."

"Stop it!" Chito laughed.

"Okay, I'll be back in a minute." Remedios turned and left his apartment.

Chito went to his bedroom and changed quickly, a grin on his face the entire time. He heard a noise and looked up. Remedios was standing there smiling at him.

"Rats. I'm too late. You're already dressed."

"Naughty girl. Are you ready to go?"

"Ready." She was carrying a bright blue sweater that matched her bright blue socks.

Chito, dressed in jeans, a dark red, long-sleeve cotton shirt, and his pork pie hat, took her hand.

"You're so cute in that hat," she said.

"Glad you like it. Let's go."

They took off walking toward Fourth Avenue. Not long after, they came to that section of the street that had several businesses, including the market and the laundromat that was being transformed into the art gallery and music venue called Clouds. Chito looked around, but he did not see the homeless man, Alexander.

They took a lazy, circuitous route around the Iron Horse neighborhood with the Clouds gallery as the center of their meandering path. Most of the time, they held hands and spoke only occasionally. They passed a very large multi-story apartment complex just to the south of the gallery.

"Looks like a lot of university students live here," Remedios said.

"Yes, it's pretty close to the campus. Frankly, I'm surprised that there aren't more of these big complexes in this area since it's close to both the university and all the nightlife on Fourth Avenue. I hope we don't see more of them in the Iron Horse neighborhood. It would mean many of the houses here would be demolished."

"That would be sad," Remedios said. "This neighborhood has been here for more than one hundred years. I would hate to see it disappear and replaced by a bunch of big apartment buildings."

"Let's go a little farther east and north. I see some lights there. We can investigate and see what's going on."

They meandered in the direction that Chito suggested. Sure enough, they quickly found a construction site lit up with security lights. It appeared that only the skeleton of the large, multi-story building had been constructed. As they came closer, they could see a large sign, more like a billboard, with an illustration of the apartment complex being built. The complex was to be called Celestial Sky Apartments. The building would have six stories, five of them dedicated to apartments.

"Nice name for an apartment complex, but my bet is that there will be so much light coming from this place that it will be hard to see the night sky," Chito said.

They approached the billboard sign so they could read the smaller print. There was a short list of companies involved in building the apartment complex, chief among them Cooke, Smith, and Johnson Associates. He looked closely at the map on the sign. The map of the bottom floor of the complex showed space for several businesses, including a coffee shop and a sandwich shop, an acupuncturist's office, a yoga studio, a small art gallery, and next door to the gallery, a business called Club Rhythm, which Chito figured was going to be a nightclub. In smaller letters, he could see, "To rent space, contact Agent Jack Davis." A phone number was included as well as a website URL.

Chito stood back. "Good. We have something to go on now."

"We do?" Remedios asked. "What is it?"

"Xochi and Li told me this guy with the name Jack Davis came to Clouds gallery before it was vandalized. He offered his services as consultant for what he called 'advertising and promotions.' He left his card. There could be a connection."

He turned and put his arms around Remedios. "I think you're bringing me good luck."

She leaned in and kissed him.

"I better take you home," he said as he pulled away. "I need to get some rest so I can follow up on these leads tomorrow. Do you have an interview tomorrow?"

"Yes. But I'll always make time for you." Remedios smiled.

Chito kissed her again. He took her hand in his, and they began their walk home to Casa Pacifica.

6 A New Foundation

Chito went to his office the next morning and immediately began a search of TPD's database to see what he could learn about the agent Jack Davis and about Cooke, Smith, and Johnson Associates, the company that was building the new apartment-business complex.

He spent more than an hour searching and found very little. Jack Davis received a speeding ticket over a year ago, but that was about it for him. No complaints against him, no arrests, not much of anything. He did find that the office of Jack Davis was located on Fourth Avenue, not the address on his card. Chito would look into both addresses. Next, he searched for and found the full names of the individual partners in Cooke, Smith, and Johnson Associates. There were no criminal or misdemeanor records for any of them, nor were there any 911 calls, or reports of break-ins or thefts at their three luxury homes in the Santa Catalina foothills. All three were obviously very wealthy.

The only exception was a fight that had broken out at a bar and restaurant owned by one of the associates, Ralph Johnson. The bar was apparently owned only by Johnson, and not a part of the "associates." Nothing new there. Just some dudes who drank too much and got into a brawl. TPD cops went in and broke up the fight. No arrests were made.

Chito did find that all three associates were involved in supporting a variety of charitable organizations and events. Posted on local news media websites, he discovered that each man could be found in videos in which he was accompanied by a spokesman for a specific charity or cause. Sometimes the financial donations were quite large, thousands of dollars. It seemed pretty obvious to Chito that these news videos had morphed into a form of self-promotion for the men who made the donations. Each man obviously wanted the world to always think of Cooke, Smith, and Johnson Associates as a bunch of good guys doing good deeds.

Chito sighed. There seemed to be no connection between these businessmen and the vandals, or with those who sent the threatening note. He wasn't even sure if the vandals and the note were connected, although he figured that there could very well be a connection. It was too convenient that a threatening note would follow a break-in and acts of vandalism. He just didn't have much to go on. Chito pressed his lips together. He'd keep looking. He would have to spread a wider net and see if he could come up with something. And he'd ask Xochi and Li again if there might be something personal for either one of them that might be a factor in this. He nodded. Yeah, keep looking, he muttered to himself.

He decided to go home, eat some lunch, and think about this. There had to be something he was missing. Focus. And maybe Remedios will be home. That would be nice. Chito headed home to his Casa Pacifica apartment.

* * *

The next morning, everyone followed the regular routine at Logan's apartment. He dropped Charlie off at his elementary school, then he went to his office at the community college. Zoey walked the fairly short distance to the high school where she had been teaching biology, and where she was soon to go on maternity leave.

Logan was first to arrive home that afternoon. He immediately retrieved the letter that Zoey had asked him to read. Settling into his favorite stuffed chair, he took a good look at the envelope that the letter came in. The return address was from Olson, Larson, and Miller, Attorneys at Law, and it was addressed to Ms. Zoey Corban. Not long after Logan and Zoey had married a couple of months earlier, she had taken the surname Corban-Reid. So the lawyers didn't know about this name change, and they probably didn't know about her marriage to Logan. But why Corban? Was that her former husband's name, and their deceased son's name, too?

He opened the letter. The same formal imprint with a return address in Minneapolis, Minnesota, was at the top of the letter. It began, "Dear Ms. Corban." His eyes moved to the first paragraph.

"If you remember, we represented you in your divorce proceedings, and also we handled probate issues regarding the estate of your grandfather, the late Jeremiah Corban." Ah, so Corban is Zoey's family name, Logan said to himself. She never took her ex's name. But she took mine, he said to himself. Corban-Reid. He couldn't help but feel satisfied at that.

Logan continued reading. "Quite recently, it came to light that your grandfather, Mr. Jeremiah Corban, had revised his will shortly before his death. He transferred a significant amount of his assets to your son, Joshua Corban Nilson. In a handwritten letter, he said he believed that Joshua would need sufficient financial assets to pay for a lifetime of medical care. The letter ends with, 'In the event of Josh's death before his mother's passing, please transfer the designated financial assets to my granddaughter who is Josh's mother, Zoey Lorraine Corban. All other assets such as real estate, business assets, cryptocurrency assets, life insurance policies, personal property, etc. should remain designated to other family members and friends as stated in my will."

Second paragraph. "Ms. Corban, we have investigated this and determined that the will revision is legitimate, signed and notarized. We cannot explain why this letter with the revision disappeared during the past years. It may have just been an accident, that is, a letter that was lost among all the others of your grandfather's papers. However, one of our investigators thinks that there may have been a family member who hid the letter so as to put himself in a better position than you to inherit a larger portion of the financial assets. It is not our responsibility to track down perpetrators of criminal activity so we set aside that concern."

Whoa, Logan thought. A lost letter? Or a letter intentionally hidden? He wondered how big these financial assets might be to foster such behavior in a family member. Logan continued reading.

"Our staff looked into this and found that your son is now deceased. This means the inheritance intended for him now goes to you. We see that you now reside in Tucson, Arizona, and you are a teacher at a local high school. Please contact us immediately with information about how we might transfer these funds to you. Best wishes." The letter was signed with an illegible signature, and the name "Frederick Larson, Attorney at Law" was printed beneath the signature.

There was another sheet of paper to be read. Logan set aside the first page and looked at the second. It was a bank statement from a Minneapolis bank with the name Jeremiah Corban at the top, then in smaller letters, the name of the law firm handling his account. His eyes shifted to the bottom of the page. The original deposit was for one million dollars. Interest on the account had increased the total amount to nearly one million, fifty thousand dollars.

Logan gasped and swallowed. He swallowed the wrong way, and he began coughing violently. His eyes filled with tears. Finally, he gained control of the coughing, and he began to breathe normally again. He sat back in his chair and tried to calm himself. Should he laugh or cry? He had no idea. Oh, my god, was all he could think. Oh, my god. Zoey was a millionaire. Oh, my god.

For nearly an hour, Logan sat quietly and stared out the window, thinking, thinking, thinking. First and foremost, he didn't want to alarm Zoey, not in her present condition. He'd have to find a gentle way to tell her about this. If there even was a gentle way. He heard a sound. The door was opening.

"Hi, sweetie," Zoey said as she entered their apartment and closed the door behind her. "What are you doing? No, let me guess. You're a philosopher, and you're sitting there thinking." She chuckled.

Logan turned to Zoey and smiled. "I can't help myself. You know how it is. There's so much to think about."

She threw her backpack on a chair. "That's okay. I think you are sexy when you think."

Logan chuckled. "You're probably the only person in the world who thinks I'm sexy, thinking or not."

"That just shows how clueless you are." She leaned over and kissed him. "Everybody thinks you're sexy."

He smiled. "Whatever. Can I get you something to eat? Are you thirsty?"

"No, my teacher pals took me out for lunch. I just drank a very large orange juice to go with some lasagna."

"Interesting combination."

"They were drinking wine, but since I'm hauling around these youngsters, I can't drink any alcohol."

"Come and sit with me." Logan moved to the sofa.

Zoey came around to sit beside him. As she sat, she noticed the envelope and open letter on the table.

"Oh, I see you opened the letter."

Logan noticed that her smile was gone. She was frowning now.

"Yes, I read the letter, and that's what I've been thinking about."

"Is it something awful?" She glanced at him.

Logan could hear the anxiety in her voice.

"No. In fact, I think most people would consider it good news. Very good news."

"How about you? Do you consider it good news?" Her frown hadn't disappeared.

"Yes, I think it's good news. But it's good news that comes with...uh...with...what should I call it? Responsibility. Yes, good news that comes with responsibility."

He put his arm around Zoey shoulders. "Shall I read it to you?"

"Yes, please do." She leaned against him.

Logan read the letter slowly. Zoey listened without saying anything. She lifted her head and looked at him. "When the original will was read, my grandfather gave me an inheritance of ten thousand dollars. I used that money for a down payment on a new car and to move all my possessions to Arizona. So this means there's some extra money?"

"Yes, there are additional funds, which were meant for your son Josh. Now those funds are yours." He glanced at her. There were tears in Zoey's eyes now.

"Want to know how much extra money there is?" he asked.

"I guess so. We'll have to think of something good to do with it. I mean, like you said, let's be responsible."

"Not 'we.' It's your money, sweetheart."

"Yes, but you are my husband and my life partner. What's mine is yours."

Logan took a deep breath. "And what's mine is yours."

"And you said it comes with responsibility," Zoey added. "You're pretty good about figuring out things, like how to be responsible."

"I hope you're right about that. Take a look at the bank statement on the next page. Look down at the end of the column to see the total amount." He handed the paper to Zoey.

She glanced down at the bank statement. "Holy shit!" she cried out.

Logan couldn't help himself. He started laughing. Soon enough his laughter turned into guffaws. He couldn't seem to stop. And now Zoey was laughing, too.

They sat together on the sofa, arms around each other, giggling. They both had tears streaming down their faces. Finally, they both took deep breaths and got control of the laughter.

"I'm glad Charlie isn't here. If he heard you say 'Holy shit!' you can count on him saying it again and again. He'd try to tell me it's an okay thing to say because you said it," Logan grinned.

"And he would giggle, just like you and I have been giggling."

They sat back in each other's arms. Finally Zoey spoke. "Okay, Mr. Philosopher. I bet you've been thinking about this."

Logan grinned. "I have indeed."

"So what do you think is the responsible thing to do with this very big pile of money?"

"I think we should honor your son's memory."

Zoey nodded. "That would be wonderful. How do we do that?"

"We could invest the funds into something that makes more money. Something good. Ethical, I mean. And then take those profits, just like the interest payments you see on that bank statement, and use the profits to give grants to anyone working on cystic fibrosis. We could create a foundation, and give money to projects working for a cure or for better treatment," Logan said.

"We could give the money in Josh's name."

Logan nodded. "Yes, Josh will be remembered."

"I like that," Zoey said. She leaned back and sighed.

"We'll probably have to hire a local lawyer or an accountant to help us figure out how to do this. Get it all set up, I mean."

Zoey nodded. "I think we'll have enough money to do that." She giggled again. Suddenly, she cried out. "Ouch!"

Logan sat up straight. "What's wrong?"

"I'm having contractions. They've been coming frequently this afternoon. That last one was strong."

"Oh, my god." Logan stood up. "Are you going into labor? Should I take you to the hospital? Oh, my god." His voice was full of alarm.

Zoey laughed. "I hope it's just Braxton Hicks contractions. Calm down, Logan."

"Braxton what? Should I call an ambulance?" He was frowning, the worry obvious on his face.

"No. Calm down, sweetheart." She reached up and took his hand. "Oh! Ouch! Another one!"

"I'm calling an ambulance."

"You're overreacting." Zoey grinned.

"Are you sure? I don't want to take any chances."

"I suggest you go down the hall, and see if Remedios is home. She'll know what to do."

Logan ran for the door, threw it open and ran down the hall to Frida's apartment.

"Remedios, are you home?" He banged on the door.

Chito's door opened suddenly. "Remedios is here with me."

Remedios appeared and stepped out from behind Chito. Her face was pink. She smiled and said, "What's up, Logan?"

"Zoey is having contractions. I want to call an ambulance, but she thinks I'm overreacting. She said to ask you to come and see what's wrong with her."

Chito was grinning now.

"No problem," Remedios said. "I'll go get my medical bag." She turned and kissed Chito. "See you later, my darling."

Chito felt his face getting hot. He glanced at Logan, but Logan was already on his way back to his apartment.

Three minutes later, Remedios appeared at Logan's open door. She knocked. "I'm here."

"Come on in," Zoey said. "I think it's just Braxton Hicks contractions."

"When did these start?"

"A week or so ago, off and on." Zoey looked at Logan. The alarm on his face was still there. She turned to Remedios. "But lately, they've been stronger and coming more often."

"How far along are you?"

"Well, it's hard to say exactly when I got pregnant. Logan and I have a very active sex life. But my doc thinks I'm about twenty-eight weeks."

Both women looked at Logan. His face was red.

"You haven't had any bleeding? Or leaking fluids?"

"No, nothing like that."

"Let me take a closer look. Or a closer listen." Remedios retrieved her stethoscope from her bag. She put the earpieces in her ears, leaned forward and put the chest piece on Zoey's chest just over her heart. Remedios listened, then moved the stethoscope to a different spot on Zoey's chest, then another spot. "Lean forward." Zoey complied, and Remedios listened to the heartbeat at her back.

"Everything sounds normal," Remedios said.

"Are you sure?" Logan blurted out. "What if there's something wrong with that stethoscope?"

"There's nothing wrong with my stethoscope," Remedios said, smiling.

"You're so patient." Zoey giggled. "Logan is sort of freaking out."

Logan frowned. "Whatever. I just want you to be safe."

Remedios moved her stethoscope over Zoey's protruding belly. She listened, moved the stethoscope around, and then sat back, smiling. "I hear two heartbeats. Very normal. Except that one of those babies whispered to me."

Zoey giggled. "Really? And what did that talkative baby say?"

"He said to tell his daddy to calm down. He said his mom is having Braxton Hicks contractions. That's all. It's very normal."

The two women looked at Logan. Both were grinning.

"Okay. Okay." He rolled his eyes and sighed.

"Zoey, I think if you get up and move around more, you won't have so many of these contractions. You won't be walking to your high school when you go on leave. So be sure to continue with your walking." Remedios looked at Logan. "Take her for some short walks, stay calm, and don't get her all upset worrying about everything. She'll know when it's time to go to the hospital."

Logan frowned. He looked at Zoey. "I'm sorry. I kind of overreacted I guess."

Zoey took his hand in hers. "Logan, I think I'm about seven months along. The babies may come a little early. That's common for twins."

Remedios nodded. "That's right. Normal gestation period for a single baby is thirty-nine to forty weeks. Twins typically are born between thirty-two and thirty-eight weeks. We want Zoey to stretch her gestation period as long as possible. Thirty-eight weeks is preferred. The babies need time to mature more before being pushed out into the world."

Logan nodded. "Okay. I get it. I'll read up on this, and I'll do my best to stay calm."

"I look forward to meeting these two babies. Do you know yet if the second baby is a boy or a girl?"

"We don't know. I kinda like the idea of a surprise," Zoey said.

Remedios nodded. She turned to Logan. "I suggest you start thinking of names. One will be for a boy. But for the second baby, you need two lists of names. One for a boy. One for a girl."

Logan nodded. "You're trying to keep me busy, aren't you? Okay, I'll be good. No more freaking out."

Zoey giggled. "Thank you, Remedios."

"My pleasure." Remedios waved goodbye and closed their apartment door behind her.

Zoey turned to Logan. "Didn't you go through this when Charlie was born? Did Caroline have Braxton Hicks contractions?"

"No. I don't think so. Maybe. I can't remember much about her pregnancy. That was nearly six years ago. All I can remember is the last day."

"The day she died?"

He nodded.

Zoey reached out and put her arms around him. "Don't worry. Everything is going the way it's supposed to go. I'm just fine, and these two babies are just fine, and Charlie is just fine, and you will be just fine, too, if you quit worrying."

Logan sighed. "Okay. I'll take your word for it."

Meanwhile, Remedios headed down the hall again and knocked softly on Chito's door.

He opened it and asked, "Everything okay?"

"Yes, no problem." She moved toward him. "Now, where were we?"

Chito pulled her into his arms, and he began kissing her passionately. He closed the door behind them.

7 Murder and Arson

The next morning, Chito was barely awake when his phone rang. TPD Chief Jake Sears was on the line.

"I hope you're ready to get started working, Detective," Sears said. "I just sent out a forensics team to look at a murder and attempted arson."

"Well, I seem to be at an impasse with this case I've been working on. Maybe it will help me to shift gears and then come back later to what I've been investigating."

"Nope. It's the same case. Or it appears to be."

'What? What do you mean?"

"The murder and arson took place at a yoga studio right next door to that gallery you were looking at. This murder-arson could very well be linked to the vandalized gallery."

"Oh, no. Who is the murder victim?"

"Probably the yoga instructor based on how she's dressed. We don't know for sure yet. I'm hoping you can identify her."

Chito felt sadness come over him. Melinda was a young women who loved her work and who loved flirting. She didn't deserve this. He sighed. "All right. It won't take me long to arrive there."

"I sent the forensics team to take photos, get fingerprints and do a preliminary check of the body. Then it will be sent to the medical examiner to determine cause of death."

Chito shook his head at the word "it." Melinda was already an "it."

"Okay. I'll contact you later this morning." Chito ended the call.

Twenty minutes later, he passed by the Clouds gallery. It was closed and the lights were off. It looked like Xochi and Li weren't early risers. He hoped he'd see them before he went back home. He walked on to the yoga studio.

Chito nodded as he passed a uniformed police officer as he entered the yoga studio. "Hey, Leah," Chito greeted the forensics officer, a middle-aged woman in a blue polyethylene-film gown and gloves kneeling next to the dead body of a young woman. Luckily, he remembered her full name. Leah Andrews.

"Hi, Chito. Chief says you may be able to identify the victim."

Chito knelt down next to Melinda. She was on her back so it was easy to see her face. Her eyes were closed. Good. He hated looking into open dead eyes.

"Yeah. I can identify her. Her name is Melinda Russell. She's the owner of this studio and a yoga instructor. I talked to her a couple of days ago. Any idea what caused her death?"

"Seems pretty obvious. Notice the blue bruise marks around her neck. And see how her head is a little off kilter."

Chito took a closer look. "Yeah, that's kind of weird. Her head doesn't line up quite right."

"I'm almost certain her neck was broken. The perp grabbed her around the neck, choked her, and twisted her head enough to sever her skull from the cervical spine. If she had survived, which was very unlikely, she would have been permanently paralyzed. The medical examiner will confirm this."

Chito shook his head. "She's so young. No more than twenty-five I would guess."

"Yeah, she didn't stand a chance. The dude who murdered her was big, and very strong."

"I'll remember that when I bring him in."

Leah grinned at him. "You always get your man, don't you, Detective?"

"So far, that's been the case." Chito shrugged.

"I heard you got shot."

"Yeah, a little bit.

"Just a little bit shot?" She chuckled.

Chito looked at her and grinned. "Turned out good for me, though. This nurse practitioner I met fixed me up. Her name is Remedios."

"Remedios? Have you had sex with her yet?"

"*Dios mío*, Leah. You ask personal questions, don't you?"

Leah laughed. "Okay. Tell Remedios that I said she needs to give you some sexual therapy so you can relax because you have a very stressful job."

Chito didn't know what to say to that, although he thought that was a very good idea.

"Or I'll tell her myself." She laughed.

"No! No need to do that! Thank you very much."

"Don't tell her. Show her!" Leah looked down between Chito's legs and wiggled her eyebrows.

"Good grief. You are really a rowdy one, Leah. I had no idea."

"That's what happens when you're over fifty. The closer I get to sixty, the rowdier and naughtier I intend to be. By the time I'm eighty, I'll be a holy terror. I spent way too many years being a nice girl. So, Chito, want to look at the evidence for an arson attempt?"

Chito sighed in relief. "Yes."

"I found signs that the perp poured out something flammable, probably gasoline. I'm guessing that from the smell at the baseline of this wall." She pointed to the interior side wall of the studio.

Chito saw immediately that just on the other side of the wall was the Clouds gallery interior wall.

"And here you see the perp broke away some of the sheet rock so the flames would go up and into the wall. Lean down here and look closely. The flames did go up a little but did not go much farther because the wall on the other side is adobe. The arsonist didn't pour any of the flammable liquid along the entire baseline either. Maybe he was in a big hurry since he'd just committed murder."

"Or maybe he was mainly interested in trying to catch the place next door on fire," Chito said.

"Why do you say that?"

"There's a new art gallery and music venue going in next door. Also an artist's studio where classes will be taught. The place has been vandalized and a threatening note was sent demanding that they shut the place down. And it's not even open yet. It opens Saturday."

"Somebody has it in for them already. Any idea why?"

"No. I've been looking into this, but I haven't found any links to anyone in particular. I suppose any or all of the galleries and clubs and bars along Fourth Avenue may not like the idea of a new place that would be even more competition for them. It doesn't seem to be anything personal with the two people opening it. By the way, they are calling it Clouds, and they are planning an opening on Saturday evening. Consider yourself invited."

"Will there be any sexy guys there who might want to go home with an older woman?" She grinned at Chito.

"Sorry, Leah. I'm not an expert on sexy guys."

"You're becoming an expert on a nurse named Remedios?"

"I'm trying."

"Ah, ha. That's what I thought. Be sure and ask what she knows about sexual therapy for very stressed out police detectives."

Chito chuckled and stood up. "Okay. Well, Leah, looks like I have a lot of work to do to catch the person who thinks it's okay to kill a young woman and try to burn down a building. And meeting you again has been entertaining. I'll seriously consider your therapy advice."

"You do that, Detective Alvarez. Later this afternoon, we'll send you an update confirming cause-of-death and anything else I find here."

Chito waved goodbye to her and walked next door. Through the window, he could see Li inside so he knocked on the door. Li came to the door and opened it.

"Welcome, Chito. How's it going?"

Chito nodded. "I have some bad news. Is Xochi here? I'd like to tell both of you."

"She's in the back trying to get everything arranged on the shelves." Li led the way.

"Hi, Chito," Xochi stopped what she was doing and waved to him.

"I want you two to know that someone went into the yoga studio next door, murdered Melinda, the yoga instructor, and tried to start a fire."

Xochi gasped, and Li said, "Oh, my god. That's awful!"

"I don't think Melinda was the target. She just happened to be there, and she got in the way." Chito gestured to the inside wall that was next to the yoga studio. "It appears that they were intentionally attempting to start a fire that would spread to your place. Luckily, there's an old adobe wall there, and adobe doesn't catch fire."

Tears filled Xochi's eyes. Li put his arm around her shoulder.

"They've taken her body to the medical examiner. I hope someone can contact her family to let them know about this," Chito said.

"I know Melinda's roommate, the woman she shares an apartment with. I'll call her," Xochi said. "Chito, I don't understand what's happening."

Chito nodded. "It's pretty clear that someone really does not want you to open this gallery. I can only guess that you are seen as a serious threat, perhaps to another similar gallery or music venue. I'm working on this full time."

Li nodded. "I think you're right about that. It doesn't seem to be anything personal directed at Xochi or me. Whoever it is just doesn't want us here. And I have something to add that I hope will help you in your investigation."

"What's that?"

"Xochi was with one of her students this morning talking about classes to be offered later this month, and I was out here doing some touch up with the paint brush. Remember that guy we told you about, the one who offered to do ads and promotions for us. The man named Jack?"

"Yeah, you gave me his card."

"He came in this morning and stayed about two minutes. He told me that we should close down immediately because someone very powerful was after us and would not tolerate us opening a new business."

"So he didn't mention wanting to do promotions for you at all? And he didn't say who this powerful person might be?"

"Definitely not. He looked scared, and he kept looking over his shoulder the entire time he was here. Like I said, he was here about two minutes. He behaved quite differently than the first time he came here."

"That's all he said?"

"That's all." Li said firmly. "It was all about someone powerful not wanting our gallery and music here."

"Maybe you should consider delaying your opening," Chito said.

"The problem is that we've invested a lot of money in this place, and a lot of time and effort into doing our own promotions for the opening. We're ready to hang the art," Li said. "Now we're seriously considering hiring a security person to be here during the opening. But it would be really great, Chito, if you could figure out who this person is and stop him."

"I'm working on it." He turned toward the front door, then turned back immediately. "Contact me if anyone bothers you or if you get anymore of those threatening notes."

"We will," Li said.

Chito started to walk home, then remembered the homeless man, Alexander. He looked across the street and didn't see him so Chito went closer to the large creosote bush where Alexander spent his nights. There Alexander was, curled up on his side, apparently asleep. As he approached, Chito saw that Alexander wasn't taking a nap at all. There was a bullet hole in his forehead. Dead. And judging from his blue skin tone, he'd been dead for a while.

"*Dios mío*," Chito muttered. He reached for his phone and called in the body that he'd just found. While he was waiting, he asked to speak to the chief.

"This is getting serious, Chief," he said. "If you remember, this homeless man I just found dead was the only one who saw the two perps break into the gallery and vandalize it. I'm going to be putting all my attention on this now. I may have to call for reinforcements."

Before Chito hung up, the chief said, "One more thing. The medical examiner took a look at the yoga instructor's body. As Leah Andrews said, she died from being choked, and then her neck was broken."

"Yeah, that was pretty obvious."

"Also the medical examiner found some DNA on the body that does not match the deceased. Male DNA."

"That could be very helpful. Okay. I'm going now. Let's stay in touch." Chito ended the call.

Two cops and Leah, the forensics officer, showed up first. They were followed by an ambulance with two attendants ready to haul the body away.

Chito left them to their work, and he headed home.

* * *

Logan hadn't been home for long when he received a text from the apartment management business that overlooked several apartment complexes in Tucson, including Casa Pacifica. "Uh oh," he whispered to himself after he read the text. He heard the door open. Zoey was home, and she smiled broadly when she saw him.

"Hello, handsome man, father of Charlie, father of our twins, love of my life."

Logan chuckled. "Hello to you, my lovely. What have you been up to?"

"After you left this morning, I called that lawyer in Minneapolis. I told him that you are my husband, and you can speak for me, too. I told him about Josh and what you and I are going to do with that money. He told me to send him a certified letter with all that information plus the name of our bank and the bank account number, and he'll work on transferring the funds."

"So we need a new bank account. I mean, we should probably have a new account just for Josh's money."

"Yes, you're right. If we want to set up a foundation, it has to be separate from our regular money. So I called our bank here in Tucson, and I told them that very soon, we'd be opening a new account and that will become the foundation's account. We can call it 'Josh's Fund.' For now, though, the money goes into our regular joint account."

"Good. 'Josh's Fund' sounds perfect. You're so efficient."

Zoey laughed. "I'm kind of amazed at myself. I'm so pregnant that I can't think straight half the time. I'm very emotional."

"Not to worry. I'll take care of you." Logan took her hand and kissed it.

Zoey's eyes filled with tears. "You're already taking care of me." She wiped away tears. "See what I mean? I'm so emotional."

"You're just fine. I love everything about you. So it sounds like all went okay at our bank."

"I warned the bank clerk here to expect a large amount of money, and he asked how much. I told him, and he gasped and started coughing like he was choking."

Logan laughed. "That happened to me, too. You should have seen me. I choked and coughed because I was so shocked."

"And then you started thinking." She kissed his cheek. "My philosopher."

Logan nodded.

"I'm going to contact the bank in Minneapolis and fill them in, too. I'll direct them to the lawyer there. The money will get transferred, and when we start Josh's Fund, we can move the money to the new account," Zoey said.

"Well done. I have a lawyer who can help us set up the foundation. Her name is Becca Rivers. She and I were in the master's philosophy program at the University. I decided to go on for my doctorate, and she decided to go to law school instead. She's a good person, and she's really smart. I already called her, and she agreed to see us."

"Sometimes I think you know everyone in Tucson," Zoey chuckled.

"Not everyone. But I've lived here a while, and I met a lot of people at the University when I was a student and a teaching assistant there."

"I look forward to meeting Becca. Meanwhile, I'll start reading up on foundations and how to run them."

"Good idea. But before we move on that, we have to figure out what to do about Charlie's birthday. I invited four of his friends over for a little party early Saturday afternoon, and Chito's daughter Isabel is coming, too."

"I bought Charlie a 3D puzzle that makes a dinosaur when it's put together. And I got a set of three linked picture story books. The first one is called 'What Do You Do With an Idea?'"

Logan chuckled. "I should read that book. I have lots of ideas, and I don't know what to do with them." He sat back and looked at her. "I have a special gift for Charlie. And it's for you and me, too. I've arranged to rent an Air B&B in La Joya on the coast just north of San Diego. We'll drive out, stay there on the coast, and go swimming in the ocean. The coastline there has wide beaches, sea cliffs, and there's even a cove where we can rent a kayak and go exploring. This will be Charlie's first time to see the ocean."

"Oh, Logan. That's a great idea! Charlie will love it. Me, too!"

"Do you think it's okay for you to take a trip like that? I'll make sure you get enough rest. You can lounge around on the beach while Charlie and I splash in the ocean."

"Yes, better we go now than later when it's closer to the time I'm due. I want to be home so I can make it to the hospital on time for the delivery. So yes, the semester is almost over, and then Charlie will have his mid-winter vacation from school. It's the perfect time. And what a great idea!"

Logan nodded. "We can visit Sea World San Diego, too. Now, about the party Saturday afternoon."

"How about if I handle the refreshments? A birthday cake and some ice cream, of course."

Logan smiled. "Sounds perfect. I have some games planned for them to play."

Zoey looked out the window. "Oh, here comes Charlie."

"I'll go open the front door for him."

Logan greeted Charlie who immediately tossed his backpack into their apartment, yelled out, "Hi, Zoey Mom!" and immediately headed upstairs.

Five minutes later, Charlie and Gwenny the greyhound came bounding down the stairs and into their apartment. Charlie was laughing loudly, and Gwenny was wagging her tail vigorously as they ran around in big circles in the living room, Charlie in the lead.

Logan looked at Zoey, sighed, and rolled his eyes. She laughed.

"Zoey, there's one other thing I need to tell you. I found out earlier today that the owners of our apartment building are planning on selling it."

Zoey's eyes went wide. "Oh! What does that mean for us?"

"I don't know. It will depend on who decides to buy it. We'll have to figure out what we'll do when we know more."

Zoey's lips were pressed together tightly. "I'm going to think about this."

"Uh oh," Logan chuckled. "You're getting the philosopher's disease."

She grinned and kissed him. "Let's go fix this boy something to eat."

Logan nodded. "Snack time."

* * *

Chito arrived back at his apartment around six p.m. He found a cold beer at the very back of his refrigerator, the last one. He really needed to go grocery shopping. He collapsed onto his sofa, popped the can open, and took a long drink. He realized that he hadn't eaten lunch, and now he was starving. Maybe he could get Remedios to come over and eat supper with him. He'd thaw out a dish or two that he'd frozen earlier.

There was a soft knock on his door, and a familiar voice. Remedios. "Chito, are you here?"

He jumped up and threw the door open. She was standing there, so beautiful, holding a plate in her hands that was covered with a cloth napkin.

"Remedios! Come in!" He knew he was grinning like a goofball. He couldn't help himself. He was happy to see her.

"Oh, I'm sorry. I can't. I'm visiting my parents this evening and eating dinner with them. I just brought you something to eat for supper." She removed the napkin.

"Tacos!" Chito said. "I love your tacos."

Remedios handed him the plate and replaced the napkin. "I made ten of them. I know you must be starving."

Chito took the plate and moved it to his kitchen table. He turned back to Remedios. "Thank you so much. But I'm disappointed you won't be eating with me." He pulled her into his arms and kissed her. And kissed her again. And again.

Remedios looked up at him, smiling. "Chito, you are a very, very, very attractive man. Stop kissing me, or I'll never make it to my parents' house."

Chito laughed. "If you insist." He let her go.

"Tomorrow evening?" she asked.

"Tomorrow evening." He nodded.

Remedios said goodbye and walked away. She turned once and looked at him intently then turned away again.

Chito watched her go, then returned to his apartment. He dug into the tacos immediately. Tomorrow evening couldn't come soon enough.

8 More Trouble

The next morning, Chito called Officer Hernandez, the replacement for Officer Peterson who was recuperating from his gunshot wound. "Can you come by and pick me up in your patrol car? You know where I live, right? This morning, we're going to do some investigating," Chito told him. "I'll fill you in when I see you."

Chito drained his second cup of coffee, pulled on his business suit jacket, and straightened his tie. He found the business card that Jack Davis had given Xochi and Li, and he looked at it closely. There was a phone number and an address on the back. The address was the same as the new multi-story apartment and businesses that he and Remedios had discovered on their evening walk. Obviously, that couldn't be the correct address since the building was far from being finished.

Chito called the phone number, and he got a recorded message that directed interested persons to an office on Fourth Avenue where they could inquire about the promotional services that Jack Davis offered. Chito was writing the address down in his notebook when he heard a sudden scream coming from the front of the apartment building.

He bolted out of his apartment, slamming the door behind him. He could see Logan ahead of him rushing out the front door and down the front steps. When Chito arrived only seconds later, he found Logan and a strange man engaged in a fist fight. He didn't know who hit first, but he saw Logan land a punch first in the man's jaw, and then his stomach. The man was struggling to get up now, red-faced and furious.

"Who the hell do you think you are?" the stranger yelled.

"I'm her husband, you piece of shit!" Logan growled.

"No, *I'm* her husband," the stranger said.

"You are *not* my husband," Zoey cried out.

"Okay. Enough of this. Stand back, both of you," Chito said loudly to the two men.

"Mind your own business!" the stranger yelled at Chito. He bent forward, intent on throwing himself forward and crashing into Logan.

Chito pulled his identification card from his pocket and moved his suit jacket back so the stranger could see his gun in its holster.

"I am Detective Julio Alvarez of the Tucson Police Department. Stand back!"

Both men stood silently, glaring at each other.

Officer Hernandez arrived at that moment in his patrol car. He pulled up against the curb and got out of the patrol car. "Need any assistance, Detective?" he asked.

"Possibly." Chito gestured to the stranger. "Ready to calm down now?"

"Yeah," the man muttered.

Chito turned to Logan and Zoey. "What is going on here?"

"He attacked Zoey!" Logan said loudly.

"I did not!" the other man yelled.

Chito looked him, eyebrows raised in warning. He turned to Zoey. "Okay. Zoey, you go first. Tell me what happened."

Zoey, eyes full of tears, pointed to the man. "That is my ex-husband. His name is Steve Nilson. He abandoned my son Josh and me when Josh was sick in the hospital." She looked at Chito. "Josh died when he was just three years old. Steve took off when Josh was sick. He didn't want to be bothered with us anymore. Not long after Josh died, I hired a lawyer, and we got a divorce. Both of us signed the divorce papers. This was several years ago."

"Logan?" Chito gestured to Logan.

"I heard Zoey scream, and I saw this piece of shit trying to grab her and pull her to his car." He gestured across the street to a parked car.

Zoey nodded her head vigorously. "That's right. I came out to water my rose bushes, and Steve showed up. He wanted me to go with him, and when I resisted, he grabbed me. Logan came out then and stopped him."

"Why are you trying to grab her? What do you want?" Chito asked.

"She owes me a lot of money!" the man was still yelling.

"I do not!" Tears were streaming down Zoey's face now. Logan put his arm around her shoulders.

"Why do you think she owes you money?" Chito asked.

"Our son got a big inheritance from a relative. I found out from a friend in Minneapolis that Zoey gets the money because our son is dead now. I was Josh's father so I deserve half that money." Nilson's face was bright red.

Chito turned to Logan. "You know about this? How much money?"

Logan spoke in a low voice. "Yes, we just found out." His voice went even lower. "A lot of money. A lot."

Chito turned back to Steve Nilson. "Looks to me like you don't get anything since you two divorced long before this inheritance came in. But I'm not a lawyer. I suggest you get a lawyer." He turned to Zoey and Logan. "You, too. You need a lawyer."

He turned back to Nilson. "However, I can say for sure that you cannot assault this woman or attempt to kidnap her. I'm going to let you go for now, and I strongly suggest you head back to wherever you came from. Don't come around here again."

The man stood there, furious.

"Now!' Chito raised his voice. "Or Officer Hernandez here will escort you for an involuntary stay in the Pima County Detention Center. Again, get yourself a lawyer and do this the legal way."

The man glared at Zoey and Logan. He did not move.

Chito gestured to Officer Hernandez who removed handcuffs from his belt and headed toward Nilson.

"Okay. Okay. I'm going," Nilson said. He headed for his car, turned back, and he growled at Zoey, "You'll be hearing from me, Zoey!" He got into his car and drove away too fast.

Chito turned to Zoey and Logan. "Think about getting a restraining order against your ex, Zoey. This is called an Order of Protection in Arizona. He'll have to stay away from you for two years or he could be arrested."

"What if he comes back right away and tries to grab Zoey?" Logan asked.

"Call Tucson Police right away. It's illegal to assault her or force her to go with him. He would be subject to immediate arrest."

"We have a lawyer now," Logan said. "I'll see if I can get her started on this Order of Protection right away. And set right the inheritance."

"Good. Okay. Officer Hernandez and I have work to do. You two stay safe. Text or call me if you have a problem."

"Thank you, Chito," Logan said.

"Yes, thank you so much," Zoey added.

Chito shook his head. "Casa Pacifica again."

"Yeah, I know. I know." Logan frowned.

"Officer Hernandez and I need to get to work. We're investigating two murders. You two be safe." He turned and joined Officer Hernandez in his patrol car.

* * *

"We're going to an office address on Fourth Avenue." Chito retrieved Jack Davis's business card from his pocket. He read out the address and, as soon as they arrived at Fourth Avenue, they both began looking for it.

"There!" Chito said, looking at a shop that had the same address as on the card. There was a staircase next to the shop that led upstairs. Officer Hernandez found a parking place, and they both left the cop car and approached the shop. The sign on the door said that the shop sold metaphysical supplies.

"What's a metaphysical supply?" Hernandez asked Chito.

"I have no idea. I see candles in the window. Maybe candles?"

They turned to the stairs. Chito could see a small sign posted on the wall of the staircase. "Look. There's the name of the man we're looking for. Jack Davis. His office must be upstairs."

They mounted the stairs with Chito in the lead.

As they approached the landing at the top of the stairs, Chito heard voices behind the door that led into Davis's office. The voices were two people, a man and a woman. He and Officer Hernandez stopped to listen.

"I didn't do anything," the man said. His voice sounded stressed, even afraid.

"Oh, but you did! You're getting in the way of my husband."

"No. No. No," the man said. "I'm trying to help him."

Chito guessed the man was Jack Davis. He had no idea who the woman was.

"You're in the way!" the woman shouted. "My husband was forced to send his men to shut down the gallery. But those stubborn trouble makers won't listen. They refuse to close it. You warned them, didn't you, Jack? Did you mention my husband's name?"

"I told them to get out of the way. I told them that there were bigger people than them who had plans for the area. I told them they would be stupid to continue. There's no way they could compete with Mr. Johnson. But I didn't mention Mr. Johnson's name. I didn't!"

Chito frowned. Li had told him exactly what Jack Davis had told him, and it was far less than what Jack Davis was saying now. Davis seemed desperate to defend himself. Chito pulled his gun from his holster, as did Officer Hernandez.

Suddenly the man squealed. "Don't shoot me!"

At that, Chito shoved open the door with his gun in hand, ready to shoot, with Officer Hernandez right behind him, ready to shoot as well.

Too late.

Just as he shoved open the door, the sound of a gunshot exploded. Chito could see a young woman with a pistol in her hand. She'd just shot the man, and Chito could see him prostrate on the floor, bleeding from a wound in his neck.

"Drop the gun!" Chito yelled.

The woman, startled, stared at him.

"Drop the gun, or I'll shoot!"

She began to cry. She dropped the gun on the floor.

Officer Hernandez jumped forward and kicked the gun out of the way.

"I didn't mean to shoot him," she whined. "It was an accident."

Whatever, Chito thought to himself. "Handcuff her, Hernandez, then call this in, and tell them we need an ambulance, too. I'll check if the victim is still alive."

Once handcuffed, Hernandez pushed the young woman down onto a chair. Only then did Chito put his gun away. Hernandez called for police reinforcements while Chito went to Davis's body. He felt for a pulse. He turned to Hernandez and shook his head. "Looks like the bullet entered his neck at an angle and went up into the brain. Likely his death was instantaneous."

The woman was staring at the body and sobbing.

"What is your name?" Chito demanded.

"Alyssa," she whimpered. "I think I need a lawyer."

Chito picked up her purse and found her wallet. Her driver's license identified her as Alyssa Johnson. He looked at her. "Ms. Johnson, I'm arresting you for murder," he said. Then he recited her Miranda rights.

Alyssa Johnson began to cry again. "Don't tell my husband. He'll be so disappointed in me. I was just trying to help."

Chito shook his head and sighed. He could hear the police and ambulance sirens coming closer while he looked for identification on the victim's body. As he thought, the dead man was Jack Davis.

Two additional police officers came and took Alyssa Johnson away, and the ambulance team took the body of Jack Davis.

"I'm going to look around," Chito said to Officer Hernandez, who stood at the top of the stairs now, ready to stop anyone who tried to come up. Chito did a quick search of Davis's desk. He found nothing of much interest until he came to a folder labeled: "Cooke, Smith, and Johnson Associates." Johnson? Did the Johnson in this business group have anything to do with Alyssa Johnson? "Don't tell my husband," she'd said. He'd check on that back at headquarters.

Inside the folder, at the very top of a pile of papers, Chito found a notice from Cooke, Smith, and Johnson Associates that the rental agreement between the associates and Jack Davis was terminated immediately. And what did that have to do with Davis going to Li and Xochi and telling them to shut down the Clouds gallery? Had Davis been threatened, and was he was trying to warn Xochi and Li?

Chito and Officer Hernandez returned to headquarters. He found out immediately that Alyssa Johnson had made her allotted phone call, and her lawyer had already arrived. Chito went directly to Chief Sears, and filled him in on what had happened. "Chief, want to come and sit in on my interview with Alyssa Johnson? I think this case is more complicated than a simple murder. For one thing, the perpetrator got her lawyer here before I even arrived back from the scene of the crime."

"Sounds interesting. Sure, I'll sit in."

When Chito and Chief Sears entered the interview room, they found Alyssa Johnson seated at the table. A man was sitting next to her.

Chito introduced Chief Sears and himself. He looked at the man. "And you are?"

"I'm Mrs. Johnson's attorney, James Lyle."

Chito looked at Alyssa. "Mrs. Johnson, please tell us why you shot Jack Davis."

Alyssa looked at her attorney, then to Chito, she said, "No comment."

Chito looked down at his notebook. "What did you mean when you said 'My husband was forced to send his men to shut down the gallery.'?"

"No comment," she said, sobbing now.

"What gallery were you talking about?"

"No comment."

"What is your husband's name?"

Alyssa sobbed even harder. "No comment."

Chito looked at Attorney Lyle. "So is this how it's going to be?"

"Mrs. Johnson is clearly traumatized. And I need some time to investigate what really happened here. It's too soon for you to be badgering her with leading questions. I'm working now to get her released to a mental health facility where she can get good care."

Chito glanced at Chief Sears. He was frowning, and Chito could see a muscle working in his cheek. Chito turned back to Alyssa Johnson.

"Mrs. Johnson, you're going back to your holding cell. Mr. Lyle, you'll hear from us again. You can go now." He and Chief Sears stood up and left the room.

Back in the main headquarters room, Chito was taken aside by one of the officers on desk duty.

"We looked into this and found that Alyssa Johnson is the wife of Ralph Johnson. He refers to himself as an 'entrepreneur' on his website," the officer said. "He's part of a business group known as Cooke, Smith, and Johnson Associates."

"Good to know," Chito said. "That helps a lot. Thanks."

He went to Chief Sears again. "We need to figure out who these two men are, the ones who work for Ralph Johnson, the ones sent to shut down the gallery."

"I'll get someone working on that. You've had a hard day, Detective. Go home. Get some rest. We'll take it from here."

* * *

Officer Hernandez dropped Chito off at Casa Pacifica. He went to his apartment, took off his suit jacket, untied his tie and pulled it off, and collapsed onto the sofa. What an awful day yesterday was, and today wasn't much better. He didn't like all these dead bodies. And no cold beer. He sighed and closed his eyes.

"Chito." The voice was soft but he heard her immediately. Remedios.

"Come in," he called out.

Remedios Davila entered his apartment, closing the door behind her, and sat down beside him on the sofa.

"You had a hard day today, didn't you? You look tired and really stressed out."

"Yes, a hard day today and yesterday, too, and yes, I'm tired and stressed." Chito took her hand in his.

"Chito," her voice demanded that he look at her. He did. Such beautiful big brown eyes.

"Chito," Remedios said again, "I think you need some therapy."

"Therapy?" He immediately thought of Leah Andrews and her suggestion that he needed sexual therapy. He couldn't help himself. He smiled.

"Yes, therapy to reduce your stress."

Chito nodded. "I guess so. I don't know."

"Yes. I want you to trust me." What's she talking about? he asked himself. Trust? He realized in that instant that he trusted her completely. "I do trust you."

"Good." She smiled. "I'm going to my apartment, and when I return, I'll be dressed differently."

"Okay." What difference does it make what she wears to do a therapy session?

"When I return, I'll be dressed differently, and I want you to be dressed differently, too."

His eyebrows went up. "Dressed how?"

"No shirt, and wearing your Minions pajamas."

Chito laughed. A wave of happiness and intense desire washed over him. He remembered what she'd said earlier about how she wanted to make love to him. She'd said, "I want you to wear your Minions pajamas so I can take them off of you."

"Really? You want me in my Minions pajamas?"

"Really. I'm going to give you a therapy session. I'll help you to relieve your stress."

Whoa! He couldn't stop smiling.

They both stood up.

"Hurry," Chito grinned. "I need your therapy. I'm desperate for your therapy."

Remedios laughed. "Back in a minute."

When she returned, Remedios was dressed only in a blue silk robe, nothing underneath. Chito, shirtless and in his Minions pajamas, was ready for her.

9 PAYBACK

Chito woke up suddenly at the sound of his phone beeping. He opened his eyes and immediately became aware of the warmth on one side of his body. He turned his head and saw that Remedios, beautiful Remedios, was curled up against him. Warm. Breathing softly. So sweet. He smiled as he reached for the phone.

The text was from the Chief of Police, Jake Sears. "Arrested 2 perps attempting gallery break-in. Interrogate this morning."

Damn. He wanted to stay here, eat breakfast with Remedios, and hold her again. He sighed, pulled himself up, started the coffee maker, and headed for the shower. After showering, he put an ice cube in the coffee to cool it a little, and he gulped it down as fast as he could.

So now Chito, dressed in his business suit and ready for work, stood over his bed and looked at Remedios who was still asleep. He wanted more than anything to get back in bed so he could, as she put it, 'take a closer look' at her. But he couldn't, due to the time pressure from his current case. He hoped that the two perps the chief texted him about were the thugs Alyssa Johnson had mentioned. Chito had to find her husband, too, assuming he could be found. Rich guys like him tended to disappear just when the cops were looking for them.

Remedios opened her eyes and looked at him. She smiled. "I love you, Chito," she said softly.

Chito stopped breathing for a moment. Something came over him, something quiet and comforting, something right. He nodded. "I love you, too." He smiled. "I have to go now, but I'll see you later." He turned and closed the door behind him, knowing that if he stayed a second longer, he'd be in bed with her again. He went out the front door of the apartment building and found Logan sitting on the steps.

"Hey, Chito. I'm waiting for Zoey. We're going for a walk. After that run-in with her ex, I've decided to accompany her on her walks from now on."

Chito nodded. "Good idea. Have you heard from that butthead again?"

"No, but I'm not taking any chances. She's getting so big now, and she certainly doesn't need some asshole manhandling her. I called our lawyer, too. How are things with you?"

Chito sat down next to Logan. "Good and bad. The good part is…" he paused. "I don't know how to say this so I'll just jump in. I'm crazy in love with Remedios, and that scares the hell out of me."

Logan laughed. "I get that. I'm scared, too, most of the time. I worry about Zoey and Charlie both, and now there are two new ones coming soon to worry about. Love does that to you."

Chito nodded, looked off in the distance, then back at Logan. "I'm waiting for one of our officers to pick me up. Things haven't been going well at work. Too many dead bodies. I'll spare you the details. So where are you two going to go walking?"

Logan gestured to the west. "I heard there was a new apartment building going in over that way. I thought we'd check it out."

"Yes, I'm familiar with it. It's going to be multi-story with shops on the ground level. It's being built by a group called Cooke, Smith, and Johnson Associates."

Logan frowned. "That sounds familiar." He was quiet for a moment then turned to Chito and said, "One of my former students came to visit me recently. She told me she was married now to the Johnson in Cooke, Smith, and Johnson Associates."

Chito's eyebrows went up. "Alyssa Johnson?"

"Yes, that's right. What a strange coincidence." Logan shook his head.

"Don't mention this to anyone, but she shot a man dead yesterday."

"Oh, my god. Seriously?"

"Yeah, we have her in custody now. We haven't figured out yet for sure why she shot this guy. Did she seem mentally stable to you?"

"Well, I'm not sure exactly what you mean by 'stable.' I'll say this. She seemed incredibly insecure and way too worried about maintaining her husband's approval. She said she wanted to help him in his business. But, obviously, killing someone isn't a good way to do that. I recommended that she see a counselor to help her deal with her insecurity, although I didn't put it quite that way."

"You may get called to testify," Chito said. "Her lawyer is claiming already that she's unstable and needs to be committed to a mental health facility, not put in prison. If Alyssa mentions you to her lawyer, you may be asked to testify that she's unstable."

"I couldn't really say that for sure. I don't know her well at all." Logan shook his head. "So sad. Alyssa is really young."

"Okay. Again, don't mention this to anyone, and let's hope your name won't come up. By the way, how's that other student of yours? The one who was drunk and singing and waving his gun around?"

"Really good, actually. He contacted me and told me he's giving up alcohol and drugs and the so-called 'friend' who gave him some kind of drug, and now he's going to start studying the Philosophy of Happiness."

Chito chuckled. "Good to hear."

The two men sat quietly again for a few minutes. Logan spoke first.

"Also I remind you that Charlie's birthday party is this afternoon. Isabel is still coming, right?"

"Yes. I'll go pick her up and bring her to the party. Sounds like a lot of fun."

Zoey appeared at that moment. "Hi, Chito. Logan is going to take his babies for a walk."

Logan stood and took her hand. "I've changed my mind. Let's go that way. We can walk over the Rattlesnake Bridge and back again."

Chito smiled. Logan was pointing the opposite direction, away from the new Johnson and Associates apartment building. Smart.

"There's my patrolman now," he said. "I'll see you two later." He rose and went to the police car.

At the TPD main headquarters, Chito found Chief Sears. "What's this about two arrests?"

Chief Sears made a quick call then turned to Chito. "I sent two patrolmen to watch the gallery last night. They were parked a little ways away in a dark area, no street lights. Around midnight, these two men showed up, dressed in black hoodies. They approached the gallery, and one of them started messing with the lock, obviously trying to break in. The other stood guard, a revolver in his hand, ready to shoot if anyone interrupted them. My men moved in and arrested them both."

"You have them both in a cell?"

"Not right this minute. I just called and told the constable to bring them directly here for interrogation."

"Any idea who they are?"

"Not for sure. But everything points to those two who were seen vandalizing the gallery."

Chito nodded. "And killed the yoga instructor, and the homeless man, and tried to start a fire."

"I want us to be able to prove that. We confiscated the gun that one perp had, and we're checking now to see if it's the same gun that was used to shoot that homeless man you talked to. We'll shoot it and see if the bullet marks match the marks on the bullet that killed the homeless man. Also keep in mind that forensics found male DNA evidence on the yoga instructor's body."

"Yes, you got DNA samples from these two?" Chito asked.

Chief Sears nodded. "We gave them glasses of water and got DNA samples from the saliva they left on the glasses." He stood up. "Let's go to the interrogation room."

The two arrested men were brought in. Chito noticed immediately that they were both tall, very muscular, and both had arrogant expressions on their faces. Unlike Alyssa, they had no lawyer waiting to represent them.

Chief Sears nodded to Chito to begin.

"You two were arrested for attempting to break into a new business that hasn't opened yet. We think this isn't the first time you've tried to get in there. Are you looking for something? Or do you just want to do damage?" Chito asked in a harsh tone.

One man did all the talking. "We weren't trying to break in."

"Why were you messing with the lock?"

"Just curious." The man speaking folded his arms across his chest and glared at Chito.

"Why were you carrying a gun?" Chito looked at the other man.

"Self-protection. I didn't want to get assaulted or robbed. That part of town is dangerous."

Chito ignored this. "Who do you work for?"

"Nobody," they both answered at the same time.

"You need to let us call a lawyer," one man said.

"Yeah," the other man added. "We don't have to tell you anything. We want our lawyer."

Chito asked a few more questions and got a "No comment" in return every time.

Chief Sears stood. "You boys are going back to your holding cell now. We'll talk about getting you a lawyer later." He and Chito went back to the chief's office.

"Won't it be interesting if the same lawyer who came for Alyssa Johnson also comes here for these two guys?" the chief said.

"Yeah, very convenient. Have you heard from Alyssa Johnson's husband, Ralph Johnson?"

"No, nothing. He's disappeared. His maid said he went on what she called an 'international trip.' But she didn't know where he was at that moment." He sat down. "That's all I need you for today, Chito. We'll have to wait until the bullet analysis and the DNA info comes in. I'll let you know what we find out."

Chito went to his desk and began searching the web on his work computer, looking for anything he could find about Ralph Johnson. There was plenty but it was all about promotion of his business, or self-promotion, telling the world what a good guy he was for supporting local charities. There was next to nothing on his personal life and nothing about his wife Alyssa. The only mention of her was a notice when she and Johnson were married, and that mention was slight. He wondered how the hell Alyssa got stuck with this man.

On his way home, Chito stopped off first to pick up Isabel. She was giggling and excited to be going to Charlie's birthday party. Her mom had taken Isabel shopping, and she had a gift for Charlie, some kind of chemistry lab, as far as Chito could tell. Isabel's mom assured him that it was age appropriate. Charlie would be able to mix solutions together to get bubbling, fizzy reactions. Chito paid Isabel's mom for the toy lab, hoping that Charlie wouldn't decide to add something extra that he wasn't supposed to add and blow up the entire building. He'd talk to Logan about the gift. They went to Casa Pacifica and found that a couple of the children had already arrived. He kissed Isabel goodbye, promised to pick her up after the party, and waved goodbye to everyone. He went straight to Remedios's apartment and knocked.

She opened the door and smiled. "Ah, my handsome man is home."

Chito said nothing. He pulled her into his arms and kissed her. "Want to come over to my place? We could... we could...do something." He wiggled his eyebrows.

"You need more therapy?" She grinned.

"Always. I'm desperate for your therapy." He kissed her again. "You are named well. 'Remedios.' That means 'remedy' or 'help.' That's you in a nutshell. My remedy." He kissed her again.

"Okay. I have to go out to my car first and get Charlie's gift. You can go with me to take it to the party. Then we'll go to your place for your therapy session."

"What did you get for Charlie?"

"A beginner's Lego set."

"He'll like that," Chito said.

"My car is parked in the lot behind our building. I'll be back in a just a minute." Remedios turned and headed for the rear exit of Casa Pacifica.

Chito went to his refrigerator first to see if he could find anything cold to drink. He ended up putting ice in a glass of water and guzzling it down. His next task was to take off his suit jacket, put his gun in its resting place on his desk, and wait for Remedios. He'd just set the gun aside and removed his holster when he heard a scream calling his name. He knew immediately that it was Remedios.

"Chito!" The scream was suddenly cut off, and her voice muffled.

He rushed out into the hall, and through the little kitchen laundry room. It took him only a few seconds to get to the back parking lot. He found Remedios in the arms of some thug, her body in a vise grip, and in the thug's hand, Chito saw a gun pointed at her head. There was a second man nearby, standing next to an expensive Mercedes. This man was dressed in casual but expensive clothing. Chito knew immediately that he was the boss, and the thug was following his boss's orders.

Chito yelled, "Let her go!" He dare not approach the man. That would just get Remedios shot and killed.

The boss man turned to Chito and smiled. "Now, Detective. No point in getting upset."

"Who the hell are you?" Chito growled.

The boss man ignored his hostility. "You've caused quite a disturbance. My wife is in jail now, thanks to you. And two of my men were arrested for doing their job."

So this was Ralph Johnson, Chito said to himself.

"Your wife shot and killed a man, and your men were caught trying to break into a business last night. And that's not the first time they've caused trouble. What the hell do you want?" Chito demanded.

"Nothing. I'm here for payback."

"What about her?" Chito gestured to Remedios. "She has nothing to do with this."

The man shrugged his shoulders. "Too bad. This woman will meet an unhappy end. Just like you, Detective. Payback."

Chito felt a tsunami of fury flood over him. He wanted to grab the man and choke him to death, but he knew if he did, the man would immediately order Remedios to be shot in the head.

"You can't get away with this. We know too much already," Chito growled.

"I can and will get away with everything you've managed to disrupt. I'm on my way to the airport, and I'll be starting a new life elsewhere. I'm going to a place where I will be treated with respect, a place that doesn't extradite to the U.S. any persecuted people like me."

"Persecuted? Don't you mean criminals?"

"I'm just a businessman, Detective. A good one. And you have disrupted my business plans."

Chito's fury turned to fear. He knew that there was no way he and Remedios were going to get out of this alive. Ralph Johnson and his thug were here to kill Chito, and Remedios would be killed, too. Johnson was out for revenge or "payback," as he put it. Plain and simple. Johnson was fleeing the country, but he wanted to make sure that Chito was punished for the investigation he'd already done, and for doing any additional investigations. Johnson was involved in something massively illegal, and Chito was very close to figuring out what exactly that was. He had to do something, or both he and Remedios would end up dead.

Suddenly, there was a loud howl coming from the man with the gun. Remedios had turned toward him slightly, and she had run her heeled shoe roughly down the man's shin from knee to ankle. The man loosened his grip, which gave Remedios the opportunity to grab and crush his testicles in her fist. He threw his arm out, the arm and hand with the gun, and he stumbled backwards, desperate to escape the pain she was causing. He tried to hit her in the face, but when he did that, Remedios quickly moved away. Chito had already jumped the distance between them and grabbed the gun.

Now Chito held the gun in a classic cop stance, ready to shoot, and to kill if necessary. "Remedios, come and stand behind me," he said. "My phone is in my back pocket. Call 911 and tell them you're calling for me. They need to come right away." Remedios followed his instructions.

Ralph Johnson opened the door of his Mercedes.

"You aren't going anywhere," Chito yelled. "Stand back or I'll shoot you."

"You can't do that."

"Try me," Chito growled.

Ralph Johnson closed the door to his car. "What do you want? I can pay you."

"I don't want your *pinche* money. I want to see you behind bars."

"Chito," Remedios said in a low voice. "I hear sirens."

Ten seconds later, two police cars came from two different directions, sirens wailing. They drove into the alleyway behind Casa Pacifica. Four cops poured out of the two police cars. Ralph Johnson and his thug were arrested immediately, and only then did Chito lower his hands with the gun in it.

He had a brief consultation with one of the police officers, gave him the thug's gun, and thanked them all. Finally, he turned to Remedios.

"Okay. So where were we?" He smiled and reached out to take her hands in his.

"Oh, you're so funny!" She laughed.

"Funny?"

"You act like this was no big deal. I was scared."

"I was scared, too. But everything turned out okay."

"Only because you're so brave! You're my hero!"

"Where did you learn that move, to scrape his shin like that?"

Remedios giggled. "It's one of the moves I learned in a women's self-defense class I took."

"Very good. And you grabbed his balls."

"He didn't like that." She grinned.

"Remind me to never piss you off." He laughed.

"Chito, I'm going to take Charlie his Legos. Meet me at your apartment in about two minutes."

He nodded and grinned. "Will do."

When she arrived back at his apartment, Remedios said, "It's absolute chaos there. The kids are jumping up and down and running around and making a lot of noise. Logan can't seem to stop laughing. Same with Zoey. And Isabel is right there in the middle of it all. She's having a lot of fun."

Chito grinned. "Good. Now I figure we have at least an hour, maybe more, before I have to fetch Isabel. Is that enough time for a therapy session?"

"Only if you stop talking!" she laughed. "Come with me!"

* * *

An hour later, Chito said to Remedios. ""Get up, lazy girl. I don't want to have to explain to Isabel what we are doing naked in my bed."

"Then let me go," she giggled.

"I can't let you go." He pulled her closer.

She sighed. "You know what your problem is?"

"No. What's my problem?" He was kissing her now.

"You're too good. You're the world's best lover. I can't resist you." She pulled away. "But I'm going to resist you, for now anyway. I'm going home and start cooking supper. You and Isabel can come and eat with me."

"Okay. If you insist."

After she'd left his apartment, Chito sat on his sofa and thought about recent events. There had to be something more complicated and totally illegal going on with Ralph Johnson. But what?

His phone rang. It was Chief Sears again. Their conversation was brief.

"First," the chief said, "we shot a bullet from the perp's gun and inspected it. The scratches on the bullet match the scratches on the bullet in that homeless man's head. That means the bullets came from the same gun barrel. Looks like we found our killer."

"And the DNA?"

"A match there, too. The DNA belongs to the other man. He's the one who killed the yoga teacher, so we're bringing murder charges against both of them. Now we're investigating the episode you were involved in this afternoon."

"Chief, I've been thinking about this. I strongly suspect that Ralph Johnson is behind everything, and his motive has something to do with money, a lot of money."

"I agree. When we took him in, we took at look at his suitcases. One of the suitcases had one million dollars in U.S. currency in it."

"What!? A million dollars!" Chito gasped.

"Yep, our officer nearly peed his pants." The chief laughed. "So I called for help from the local FBI office. They are going to use their forensic accounting team to look into this. The crime could be embezzlement, or money laundering, or some other financial malfeasance. I'll let you know what they discover."

"So I'm off this case now?"

"Yes, we'll take it from here. You can enjoy your life... for a little while, anyway." Chief Sears chuckled.

"Thanks, Chief." They said goodbye to each other, both satisfied.

* * *

Despite all the criminal activity that proceeded the Clouds gallery opening, the event went off as planned. A big crowd came, Xochi sold several pieces of art, and Li was a hit, too. He decided he wasn't ready to "take the stage," as he put it. So he sat in a corner and played his guitar for about two hours. More than once, a small crowd gathered to listen, and when he finished a piece of music, they applauded.

Logan watched all this, a smile on his face. He was happy for Li, who had a new life now as a food truck chef and a musician. And he and Xochi seemed very happy together. He looked around to make sure Charlie was behaving. His son was trailing Zoey around, looking at the art on the wall and introducing himself to anyone who would listen. His son was gregarious, he liked everyone, and he would probably end up doing something people-oriented. Logan stopped his musing when he realized that Chito was standing next to him.

"Isabel tells me that Charlie's birthday party was a lot of fun," Chito said.

Logan grinned. "Yes, fun for everyone, including Zoey and me. We laughed all afternoon. Those six year-olds were running around like crazy little monkeys. Where's Isabel?"

"Over there with Remedios listening to Li's music. Logan, I want to mention that I'm a little concerned about Isabel's gift for Charlie. I hope he doesn't blow up everything."

"Not to worry. I read the instructions, told Charlie what not to do, and I'll be sure one of us is there watching when he does the experiments. Actually, I think it's a good gift. Maybe he'll get interested in learning some chemistry. How about you? I heard about that confrontation in the parking lot."

"All settled now. Those two were arrested, and they're in jail now. They won't be going anywhere for a long, long time."

"I'm so glad you and Remedios are okay. Seriously."

Chito felt himself getting hot. He was sure he was blushing at the mention of her name.

Logan chuckled. "So how's it going with you two?"

"I'm sort of lost. I know what to do when someone points a gun at me, but when it comes to Remedios, I don't have a clue. I'm crazy about her, but I'm still scared, and I don't even know why I'm scared."

Logan chuckled. "Then go step-by-step. Spend time with her doing different things. After a while, you'll see the way open, and you'll know what to do. That's how it happened with Zoey and me. I was scared shitless. But, somehow, everything worked out just fine."

Chito nodded. "I like that. Step-by-step."

Both men looked around to make sure their kids were okay.

"Guess I'll take Isabel back to my apartment. It's almost bedtime," Chito said.

Logan nodded. "Same here. Charlie will crash soon, and I don't want to have to carry him home. He's growing super fast, and he's getting really heavy."

The two men shook hands and parted. Each went to find his child.

10 Eight Weeks Later

Logan sat in the side yard of Casa Pacifica Apartments with a book in his hand, but he wasn't reading. He was thinking, thinking, thinking about the many, major, huge, life-changing events of the past two months. Those twin babies and Charlie were the center of his life with Zoey. He loved them all more than words could say, but he wished like crazy that he could get enough sleep. Zoey tried to reassure him that the twins would start sleeping through the night soon. The average was four months, she said, and two-thirds slept through the night by six months. Sometimes Zoey made Logan go sleep on the sofa so he could actually sleep. His missed her, but uninterrupted sleep was a real relief. He sighed. He was trying to be patient. Meanwhile, he was spending regular time with Charlie so his son wouldn't feel left out because of all the attention on the twins. He and Zoey even got some alone time when Charlie was at school and the babies were sleeping. Those were his favorite times.

The sun was going low in the sky, and the temperature was dropping, too, very typical of a late Sunday afternoon in January. It was almost time for the Sunday potluck.

Chito came out the back door of Casa Pacifica and settled next to Logan in a lawn chair. They sat together in companionable silence for a few minutes.

"We're lucky we have women who like to cook," Logan said. "We're off the hook."

"Yeah." Chito grinned. "Good thing because I can't boil water. Isabel is in there with Remedios and Zoey and Angela learning how to make edible food. It's non-stop giggling. Girl talk."

More companionable silence, then Logan spoke again. "Chito, I've been wondering what happened to that rich bastard who threatened to kill you and Remedios."

"We got help from the FBI's accounting forensics. Just as my chief and I thought, Ralph Johnson was a world-class thief. He'd been siphoning money off the business he was in with those other two guys. He had an accountant in the business who was in on his theft. If you remember, the business, Cooke, Smith, and Johnson Associates, had purchased that huge lot over near Fourth Avenue, and they began construction on a multi-story luxury apartment and business building."

"Yeah, I remember seeing it. I'd guess maybe it was only twenty or twenty-five percent built when all this happened."

"Right. When we arrested Johnson and his thug, and we started looking into this, we had to inform the other two partners that there wasn't enough money to finish the construction. Hell, there wasn't enough to build another day. They couldn't pay the workers, much less get more building materials. Johnson had absconded with all that money meant for construction. Did I tell you that he was carrying a suitcase full of U.S. currency? One million dollars."

"Whoa!"

"And that wasn't all. The FBI found that he'd been transferring funds to a bank in Havana, more than ten million dollars. We found evidence that he'd acquired a Cuban visa, and he already had some business contacts there as well as the bank account. The key factor is that there is no extradition treaty between the U.S. and Cuba. So he could live the high life there without worrying about being extradited and tried for multiple crimes. He was on his way to the airport when he confronted me."

"Do you know what Johnson plans to do about my former student Alyssa, his wife?"

Chito shrugged. "I don't know what his original plan was, but when he discovered she'd been arrested, he abandoned her. Just walked away. He only had one air ticket out of the country. As for Alyssa, she's still incarcerated in a facility for the mentally ill. She was more than insecure, Logan. She was diagnosed as severely depressed and suicidal."

Logan shook his head. "So sad." He paused for a moment. "What about the Clouds gallery? Why was Johnson so eager to see it shut down?"

"Johnson had promised the building that Clouds is located in now to the accountant who was helping him embezzle funds. Back when it was for sale, Xochi and Li purchased it before Johnson could get to it. His plan was to buy it and turn it over to the accountant right away. I don't know what the accountant planned to do with the building, but by then, Xochi and Li had big plans and were starting to implement their plans."

"If Johnson had all that money transferred, and if he was on his way to the airport, why did he come here?"

"Payback. I got in his way, I caused him a lot of trouble, and he wanted to see me dead before he left the U.S. Remedios just happened to be there. She was getting Charlie's birthday gift out of her car when Johnson and his thug showed up. Johnson would have killed her, too."

"Oh, my god." Logan looked at Chito. "I don't know what to say. That's really terrible."

Chito smiled a tight smile and shrugged. "It's all over now, Logan. You don't have to worry. Those criminals are in jail, Xochi and Li have a successful gallery, Li is doing well with his food truck, and everybody loves his music. And Remedios and I…," he paused. "So it all turned out well."

"We're going to have a lot to talk about after the potluck tonight. Big changes are coming."

"Yes, I know about some of the changes." Chito smiled. "Remedios and me. We're a couple now. Step-by-step."

Logan nodded. "I better make sure that Gwenny the greyhound comes to the potluck. We want Charlie and Isabel distracted by that dog that they love so much. We'll be able to talk if they are playing with Gwenny."

"It's getting dark. I guess we'd better go in," Chito said. Both men stood up.

Logan reached out and took Chito's hand. "I'm really so glad you survived. Seriously, bro."

Chito nodded. "Me, too. Thanks for all your help."

They went into Casa Pacifica together and entered Logan and Zoey's apartment.

* * *

The Sunday potluck dinner was a fun event for all. The tenants living in Casa Pacifica were happy to welcome back Nina Perry and Gwilym Havard who had come all the way from Vancouver, B.C. to attend Tucson's January Jazz Festival. As they were putting dishes of food on the table, there was a knock at the door. Much to everyone's surprise, past tenants Cass Cosay and Dylan Scott joined them, having come from the White Mountain Apache reservation north of Tucson.

"Oh, my goodness." Zoey smiled broadly. "Our family is here! All of us!"

Cass and Dylan were welcomed as warmly as Nina and Gwilym had been welcomed. The dinner was noteworthy both for good food and a lot of laughter.

After everyone had eaten, the table was cleared, and they had all found a place in the circle of friends, Zoey turned to Charlie and said, "Charlie, would you like to introduce our newcomers?" She pointed to a bassinet that held two infants.

Charlie stood up and said to the group. "I'm the big brother." Everyone grinned and clapped. Charlie pointed to one infant. "This is my sister. She's a girl. Her name is Hope. And that's my baby brother. His name is Corban."

"Let me explain about the names," Zoey said. "Logan chose Hope because we all need and want hope. We think she'll be an inspiration for us. And as you all know, I used to be Zoey Corban. When Logan and I got married, I called myself Zoey Corban-Reid for a while. Then I thought to myself that I wanted us all to have the same name so now I'm Zoey Reid. Then Logan suggested our baby boy should be called Corban. I looked it up. The name has different meanings, but it basically means 'raven.'"

"The raven is my favorite bird," Logan said. "Ravens are really smart."

"What do you think about being a big brother?" Angela asked Charlie.

"I think it's fun. I like to play with them. I have to be careful now because their heads kind of wobble, and they can't throw a ball or anything. I'm going to show them how to play ball."

"You're doing everything right," Remedios said. "Their heads will stop wobbling after a while, then they will be able to hold up their heads by themselves. You're taking good care of your brother and sister, Charlie."

Charlie grinned.

Logan spoke now. "Okay, Charlie, you and Isabel take Gwenny with you to your bedroom. You can read Gwenny a book or she can watch you two build something with your Legos. If you get tired of that, you can come back to the living room, and the three of you can play ball."

Charlie and Isabel jumped up, called Gwenny, and the three of them disappeared into Charlie's room.

"So, Zoey, how did Logan do during the birth of these babies?" Remedios asked.

Zoey giggled. "He turned white. I was afraid he was going to pass out."

"I did not turn white!" Logan frowned. "Remedios, I thought she was going to crush the bones in my hands."

"I pulled on his hands so I could push the babies out." Zoey giggled.

"She pulled really hard." Logan rolled his eyes. "Enough of this. We have a lot to talk about. First, I want to welcome Nina, Gwilym, Cass, and Dylan, who seems to be expecting."

"Expecting one, not two." Cass grinned.

Dylan patted her protruding belly.

Logan nodded. "Watch out, Cass. She'll try to crush your hands. Okay. I've talked to you all individually, but now it's time to give you the big picture. I think we all touched base with Frida when she was here a week ago. Remedios, want to fill us in?"

"My sister has been out in the Los Angeles area involved in labor organizing. She met this man named José. He's a labor organizer, too. They fell for each other so they decided to live together and devote themselves to raising a ruckus." Remedios grinned.

"I've never seen Frida so happy," Nina said. "She's really in love."

Logan continued. "I've told most of you, or maybe all of you, that there was a plan by the real estate management company to sell Casa Pacifica on behalf of its owners."

Li groaned. "I don't want to move."

"There will be some changes, but it doesn't mean you'll have to move," Logan said. "So Xochi, Li, want to tell us what's up with you?"

"We're doing great. Everyone is crazy about Li's music." She patted his knee.

"And everyone is crazy about your art, Xochi." Li took her hand in his. "Xochi is also teaching classes in her new studio and doing her art there. I'm thinking seriously about forming a trio, with piano, percussion, and me on guitar. And my food truck is doing well, too. Because of all this, Xochi doesn't really need the two-bedroom apartment anymore. So Xochi is moving in with me in my one bedroom."

"We're going to share Li's bed," she giggled. Li kissed her.

"Angela and Marc?" Logan looked their way.

"We have a good life," Marc responded. "Angela likes her veterinary position. I like being lazy and doing nothing."

"Oh, stop it. You are an excellent photographer." Angela punched Marc on his shoulder. "He's showing his work in galleries now. And we're going to Mardi Gras soon."

"Logan, we were wondering if you could take care of Gwenny while we're gone?" Marc asked.

"Sure. I'll take her for long walks. Charlie can help me."

"That will make Gwenny happy for sure," Marc said.

"Okay. Who is next?" Logan asked. He looked at Cass and Dylan.

Cass had abandoned his former life as an FBI Special Agent, and now his long, dark braid made him look much more like the Apache tribal member that he was. "We've had some success already with our equine therapy program. We've hosted military vets and disabled children. I feel good about what we're doing."

Dylan nodded. "And Cass is going to become a father. Our baby is due in March."

Zoey blew Dylan a kiss, which Dylan returned to her.

"Nina and Gwilym?" Logan asked.

"We're at the Tucson Jazz fest," Gwilym said. "Nina's upcoming show is sold out."

Nina's eyes filled with tears. "I love you all. I especially love Cass, Logan, and Gwilym who prevented that nut case from smashing my hands and breaking all my bones. I wouldn't have been able to play piano ever again. And I love Gwilym because he's…" she paused. "Well, let's just say that he's the sweetest, kindest man I've ever known. And he's a good lover. No, a great lover."

Everyone laughed.

"Thank you, that's nice coming from a girl who is a great lover, too." Gwilym kissed her.

Logan turned to Chito. "Want to tell us what your plan is?"

Chito was stricken with sudden embarrassment. "Uh …well…" He looked over at Remedios.

"Chito is the love of my life. I adore him," she said, a huge smile on her face. "He's brave and kind and reliable and smart and, oh my god, talk about great lovers."

Chito's elbows were on his knees now. He bent his head forward and covered his face with his hands.

"But for some reason, this really smart and brave Tucson police detective gets embarrassed easily, especially when I talk about his prowess as a lover. So I'll let him off the hook. He's moving upstairs into Xochi and Li's old two-bedroom apartment. And I'm moving in with him."

Chito put his hands down and took a deep breath. "I thought it would be good for Isabel to have her own bedroom."

"Because we don't want her to see us naked and rolling around in our bed."

Everyone was laughing now.

Chito shook his head. "I just have to say that criminals are a lot easier to deal with than Remedios. They know that there's some occasions when you need to keep your mouth shut." He turned to look at her and shook his head.

Remedios giggled and zipped her lips with her finger tips. But five seconds later, she said, "Oh, wait! One more thing. I have a new job working for a local group that provides aid to migrant asylum seekers. I provide medical care, and I get to use my Spanish. I love my new job."

"Very good, Remedios. You'll be of great help," Logan said. "Here's our big news. You know that Zoey came into some money. We are doing two things. We started a foundation in memory of her son Josh. Zoey can tell you all about that. And we used part of the money she received as an inheritance to buy Casa Pacifica."

Gasps all around, then laughter, then clapping.

"We're going to pretend we have a mortgage on this place," Logan continued. "Each month, we'll pay what's equivalent to a mortgage payment to the foundation, and eventually, money we took from the inheritance to buy Casa Pacifica will go back into the foundation."

"Since I'm on leave from my teaching job, I'm going to put my attention into building the foundation. We're calling it Josh's Fund. The focus will primarily be on cystic fibrosis and other genetic diseases," Zoey explained.

"Well done," Angela said. Everyone nodded in agreement.

Logan continued. "So upstairs Chito and Remedios and sometimes Isabel will be in the two-bed room apartment, Xochi and Li in Li's apartment, Marc and Angela in their apartment, and there will be one apartment open, possibly to be rented to someone new. Downstairs, the apartment Chito is in now will be our guest apartment when we have guests, like you, Nina and Gwilym, or you, Cass and Dylan. We're hiring a construction team to do a big remodel on our apartment. We're planning on opening the wall that is now between our apartment and Frida's old apartment. We likely put a door there, too. Eventually, with the remodel, the entire west side of Casa Pacifica on the lower floor will be ours. Charlie is in one bedroom, and the twins will go in the other when they are a little older. And Zoey and I will be in the third."

Zoey interjected, "Now they are really tiny babies, so they're staying in a crib in our bedroom."

Logan nodded. "No one has to move out, although Chito and Remedios will be moving upstairs."

"Frida took a bunch of her belongings with her," Remedios said, "and I'm packing up the rest and shipping it to her. As soon as I get that done, and my own stuff moved upstairs, then Frida's apartment will be free for the construction workers to get started making her apartment part of Logan and Zoey's bigger apartment."

Logan was satisfied to see how pleased everyone was. He liked it that his own family would have more room.

The current residents would stay, and there would be a guest room for former residents. He looked around the room. Everyone was smiling.

After another half hour of conversation, Chito stood up. "It's been great talking with you all. I have to get Isabel back to her mother so she can go to bed. She has school tomorrow."

Logan stood up, too. "Same here. Charlie needs to go to sleep."

Sunday potluck broke up after a lot of hugs and kisses.

The clock on the wall said almost ten p.m. when Logan looked at it. He was the only one up. Charlie was asleep, and even Zoey had gone to bed early. That's when he heard the buzzer to the outdoor entrance. He left his apartment and went to the front door where he saw a young man, maybe mid-twenties, standing there. Logan opened the door.

"Hi, my name is Rafael. Sorry to be so late, but I just got off work. I didn't want to miss this opportunity. I heard you have an apartment coming open for rent soon."

Logan nodded. "I'm Logan Reid, the apartment manager. Come in."

Thank you and some Information Sources:

Hello Reader!

Thank you for reading *A Closer Look*, the fifth Iron Horse Mystery.

You can learn more about the Philosophy of Happiness that Logan shared with his former student here:

https://en.wikipedia.org/wiki/Philosophy_of_happiness

And if you are visiting Tucson and you are hungry, you'll be pleased to know that Tumerico is a real place to enjoy vegan vegetarian Mexican food. https://www.tumerico.com/ Of course, Tucson is a UNESCO World City of Gastronomy. There are several great places to eat. Learn more here:

https://tucson.cityofgastronomy.org/

https://www.visittucson.org/eat-drink/city-of-gastronomy/

Please leave a review of this book wherever you buy books (Amazon, Kobo, Nook, Apple, etc.) and also at Bookbub and Goodreads. By leaving a review for others to read, you can make it much easier for mystery readers everywhere to find this book.

Please sign up for my monthly newsletter all about art, books, and the natural world at www.cjshane.com/contactnewsletter.html

TRY THIS!

KISSED: CAT MIRANDA MYSTERY #1

1 THE INTRUDER

Cat Miranda's eyes opened suddenly. A noise. Downstairs. Then silence. Maybe she had imagined it? No, there it was again.

She held still in her bed, almost not breathing. Her heart began to hammer in her chest. She could hear the sound of a key or something metal being thrust into her backdoor lock and jiggled noisily.

Someone was breaking into her home and her art gallery! Cat could barely control her trembling and shallow breath. She sat up, and looked at her bedside clock. Midnight. She'd been asleep an hour or so.

What the hell? She'd only been back in Bisbee for two days. She had been almost overwhelmed with exhaustion after driving nearly four hours from Phoenix, then hauling her luggage and a couple of boxes into the living quarters above the art gallery. That was tiring enough, but she was also struggling to manage all the things that her new life would bring her. That included opening the gallery again. Meanwhile, she was dealing with intense grief over the death of her brother. It was almost more than she could handle. She frequently found herself in tears.

And now a break-in? Too much! She fought back tears and struggled to control her fear. She had to deal with this and deal with it now. She threw the bed covers back, slipped out of bed and crept to her bedroom door. Now she could hear the door downstairs opening and the sounds of someone entering her house. Oh god. What to do? She was filled with alarm.

Cat reached for the baseball bat she kept nearby in the corner of her room. She silently opened her bedroom door and crept onto the landing at the top of the stairs. There were two light switches on the wall, one for a light behind and over her head, and one in the ceiling directly above the back door. She flipped on the light above the back door as she stood still in the darkness of the landing. At the same time, she lifted the baseball bat in her two hands.

The light coming on revealed a man standing inside her house at the open back door. He was shrugging off a backpack, and at the same time, pulling a small suitcase on rollers into her house. He stopped when the light suddenly came on. He looked around, eyes squinted.

"*Merde*," he muttered in an irritated voice.

"What the hell are you doing breaking into my house?" Cat said loudly. She tried to control the trembling in her voice. She was scared, but she didn't want the intruder to know it.

The man looked up at her, seeing her for the first time. He was still squinting, trying to adjust to the sudden bright light in his eyes.

"I'm not breaking in. I have a key," he said roughly. He held up the key in his hand.

"You have an accent," Cat blurted out.

"I can't help that. I'm English," he growled.

"Okay, smart ass. Where did you get a key to my house? And why are you here?"

"I rented a room in this place for two weeks from a chap named Luis Miranda. He gave me the key. Where is he? And who the hell are you?" The man was obviously irritated. His eyes were open now and staring at her. He was scowling.

Cat felt a pain in her chest at the mention of Luis, a pain in her heart.

"I'm Cat Miranda. Luis was my brother."

"*Was*? What do you mean *was*?"

"Luis died nearly a month ago."

The man's voice changed. "Oh, I'm sorry." His tone was completely different now. He sounded genuinely sympathetic. "What happened? Was there an accident?"

"No, he was really sick. He never got better. I took care of him until the end."

"I am very sorry. I arranged this rental about six months ago. I didn't know he was ill."

"What are you doing here?"

"I'm a visiting scholar doing research. I'm close to the end of my journey so I'll be going home in a couple of weeks. I decided to spend my last days in this lovely little town near the border."

"Oh." That made sense. Cat agreed with him that her childhood home, Bisbee, Arizona, was indeed a lovely little town in the Mule Mountains of southern Arizona. The international border at Naco was only a few miles away. Bisbee had been a mining town for a long time, but now the Copper Queen Mine was open only for tours. Bisbee had become an arts and music destination.

She made a sudden decision the way she usually made them. Hers was a spontaneous, gut decision based on intuition. He seemed okay. If this guy was telling the truth, and he seemed to be, Luis had trusted him. If Luis trusted him, then Cat could trust him. Cat decided to let him in, just hoping she wouldn't regret it later. She'd keep an eye on him just in case.

"You wait there. I'll be right down."

"As you wish, m'lady."

M'lady. Well, she'd never been called that before, Cat thought.

The man stuck the key in his pocket and began rubbing his eyes with one hand. She thought he looked tired.

Cat disappeared into her bedroom and came out in seconds with a long-sleeve t-shirt pulled over her gown. She had clogs on her feet, too, as she came down the stairs. Gesturing to the man to enter the kitchen before her, she turned on the kitchen light. The baseball bat was still in Cat's hand.

"You behave yourself or else," she said.

"You'll find that I am a really nice bloke, and my behavior is exemplary."

"Bloke," she repeated, shaking her head. "Sit down. Do you want something to drink? You can explain why you're here."

"Hot tea would be welcome." He sat down at the small kitchen table.

Cat put the pot on the stove to heat water. "I don't have any of that English black tea. Will you drink tea that relaxes you and reduces tension?"

"Yes. It seems that we could both benefit from a reduction in tension."

"So who are you? What's this about being a scholar? And tell me about renting a room here." Cat looked the man over. He was tall, slim, and maybe about thirty years old. He had ruffled strawberry blond hair, and there was a little stubble on his face, as if he hadn't shaved for a day or two. His eyes were blue. Very blue. And he was handsome. Yeah, *muy guapo*, she thought to herself.

"My name is Miles Trevelyan. I'm from Sussex. That's on the south coast of England. I've been living in Oxford for several years. When I return home, I'm going to be conducting some seminars at the University of Exeter in Devon next month. I'll be working on a book, too."

"So you came to the U.S. to do research? What are you studying?"

Miles nodded. "The Borderlands. I started in the Rio Grande Valley in Texas and worked my way west all the way to San Diego. I went back and forth across the border as I progressed. I conducted a lot of interviews and took many photos as well as collecting documents. I stopped in here briefly on my way west. I liked Bisbee so much that I decided it would be a great place to decompress before going home. I thought I could start organizing material for my book here, too. Do you have Wi-Fi here? I forgot to ask your brother."

"Yes. We have Wi-Fi."

The water in the pot was hot now. Cat retrieved two cups, put a tea bag in each and filled each cup with hot water. She placed a cup in front of Miles Trevelyan. She sat down at the table across from Miles, put a cup on the table in front of her and a saucer between them for the tea bags. She handed him a spoon.

"Your name is Cat?"

"Catalina Amalia Miranda. You can call me Cat."

"That's a very pretty name. Your brother spoke about you."

"He did?" Cat felt that pain in her heart again.

"Yes. Luis told me he has….had a very sweet baby sister. He said he hoped I would get a chance to meet her …you." Miles's voice was gentle.

Cat's eyes filled with tears. She nodded.

"I came through here and spent the night at the Copper Queen Hotel. I asked around about long-term rentals. It seems that someone knew someone who knew someone who had been talking to Luis. The person I talked to said he thought Luis was considering renting out a room as a trial B&B. So I showed up here. The gallery was open so I looked around while he was talking to some customers. He sold a small painting to them. Then he and I talked about me renting his extra room for a brief time before I return home."

"He never told me."

"If he was ill, he probably had other things on his mind."

Cat nodded. "Luis had pancreatic cancer. He'd had the symptoms for some time. Persistent pain in his stomach, fatigue, weight loss. He ignored it. He was happy running the gallery, and I think he wanted to think about all his upcoming projects, not about being ill. But finally the pain got bad enough that he went to the doctor. He was diagnosed, but even with treatment, it was too late. About a month ago, I came back to Bisbee and took care of him. That way he didn't have to go to hospice. He could die at home."

Miles nodded. He frowned slightly. "Sad."

"So I guess he made those arrangements with you several weeks before he became so ill?"

"Yes, I think you must be right about that."

"I have been living and working in Phoenix since I finished college. I came back home to Bisbee frequently. Luis and I had some heart-to-heart talks on those visits. He and I decided together that we'd be co-owners of the gallery and that I would move back here and run the gallery with him. Then he became ill. When he was sick, he never spoke about death. I realize now that he knew he was dying. He was doing what he always did. He was taking care of his little sister and helping me have a better life."

"You don't think you'll miss Phoenix?"

"No. My life will be better here."

"What kind of work did you do in Phoenix?"

"I'm a graphic designer. I design stuff for businesses like logos and promotional material, advertisements and all that. Also I designed a lot of websites for businesses. I designed our gallery's website, too."

He nodded.

"I'm not really a big city girl," Cat continued. "Phoenix is big. And it's really a lot hotter in the summer than it is in Bisbee." She didn't mention that she also was escaping what she thought of as "man trouble" in the form of her ex-husband.

"Yes, Bisbee is a mile high. Much higher elevation so you have cooler temperatures."

"That's right. So, anyway, after he died, I returned to Phoenix for nearly a month. I had to quit my job and clean out my apartment so I could move back home. Luis had dreams for the gallery. He gave those dreams to me, and now they are my dreams, too. I'm going to try to make them come true."

Miles sipped his tea. "This is surprisingly good tea," he said.

"It's Mexican *manzanilla* tea. Or they call it 'chamomile' in English. Maybe it will help you to sleep better."

"Speaking of which, any suggestions where I could sleep tonight? Know of any cheap hotels or motels?"

Cat paused and stared at her cup of tea. She knew that this weekend was an especially busy one in Bisbee. There was a music festival going on for two days so she knew all the town's hotels and B&Bs were full. He'd probably have to drive twenty miles to the town of Sierra Vista to find a motel. Or go across the border into Mexico and look for a hotel. It was late at night, and that would make the search more difficult.

"Oh, all right. You can stay here," Cat said. She looked at him and said sternly. "I think you are probably okay. I've decided to trust you."

"Good decision. Like I said…."

"Yeah, I know. You're a nice bloke. Okay. Just behave yourself. I've had it up to here with obnoxious men."

"I'll be on my best behavior, m'lady. I promise." He smiled again.

Cat put the two cups in the kitchen sink. "Come on with me, and I'll show you to your room."

Miles followed her up the stairs, bringing his backpack and luggage with him.

At the top of the stairs, Cat opened the door to the room opposite hers. She turned on the light.

"This is Luis's old room. You don't mind sleeping in a room where someone died, do you?"

"No, not at all. This happens a lot in England anyway. We're an old country, and lots of people have died here and there."

So Miles Trevelyan was a smart ass with a peculiar sense of humor, Cat thought to herself.

"Let's get some sleep now, and we'll talk in the morning. Sorry about all the confusion."

"Thank you for allowing me to stay. Good night, m'lady."

Cat went downstairs and checked to make sure the back door was locked. She returned to her room and closed the door. Just to be sure, she jammed the back of a wooden chair under her door knob. She went back to bed feeling even more exhausted than before.

* * *

This time Cat was awakened by sounds that were much louder and much nearer. She opened her eyes and sat up in bed. She glanced at the clock. Three in the morning. She could hear thumping and a crash. Then she heard what sounded like Miles Trevelyan yelling at someone.

"Get out! Now!"

There was no response to his yelling, but the sounds of a struggle continued for a few more seconds. Suddenly everything went quiet.

Cat opened the door to her room, baseball bat in hand. "Mr. Trevelyan?"

The door to Luis's room flew open. Miles was standing there in a t-shirt and pajama pants, bare-footed.

"Look at this. Hurry."

He stepped aside and pointed to the open floor-to-ceiling glass door on the other side of the room. It led out onto a deck with a stairway that went to the ground floor. The screen on the door had been ripped off.

Cat hurried to the open doorway and looked down. Miles was right behind her. She could see a form dressed in dark clothing running away down the street from her house toward the main road of Tombstone Canyon.

"Oh my god," Cat whispered.

"You had an intruder. Has this happened before?"

"No," Cat said. "Never. We've never had a break-in downstairs either."

Miles turned on a lamp, and a soft light flooded the room. He reached over and put a chair upright that had been knocked over in the struggle.

"I had the glass door open so I could enjoy the cool night air. I sleep better when it's cool. Then I woke when I heard him trying to get the screen door open. I jumped up just as he came into the room. He rushed me and we struggled. He knocked over the chair. I yelled at him, and he backed up, turned and ran away."

"It was a man?"

"Yes, maybe a little heavier built than I am. Maybe not quite as tall as me but almost."

"Are you okay?" Cat looked at Miles. The lamp light revealed a dark mark above one of his eyes.

Miles reached up and touched the spot. He grimaced. "I guess he hit me. Ouch." He looked at his fingers that had just touched the wound. "There's blood."

"Come with me, and let me take a look at you."

She led him to the bathroom which opened onto the landing between her room and Miles's room. She turned on the light in the bathroom.

"Here. Sit down on the toilet seat."

Miles followed her instructions. He sat quietly with his hands on his knees.

Cat bent over to take a look. "Yes, looks like a small cut. Not deep. It's not bleeding anymore. Let me clean it up and put a little bandage on it." She turned and reached into the cabinet over the sink to retrieve hydrogen peroxide and a box of bandage strips.

She gathered some tissue into a wad and began cleaning the cut with hydrogen peroxide. She carefully placed the bandage strip over the cut. She stood back and looked at his forehead.

"Does it hurt?"

"No, not really." He was grinning.

"Why are you smiling?"

"The life of a scholar can be pretty quiet and uneventful. My trip has gone well. No problems at all. Now here at the end of the trip, I've had a chance to fight off a bandito. This little incident will make a great story to tell to my mates at the pub over some beers."

"Bandito?" Cat shook her head. "We're not in Mexico."

"Almost Mexico."

"Okay. Whatever. I'm glad you're happy. I'm not."

"No, I guess not." He looked up at her.

"I don't know why someone tried to break in here. I don't know what they want. This is making me nervous," she paused. "Also, I feel bad for you."

"For me?"

"Yes, you think you are renting a quiet room in a quiet home in a quiet town so you can wind down before you go home. The first thing that happens is an intruder breaks into your room, you get in a struggle, and you get hurt. I'm not being a very good host, am I?"

Miles shrugged. "Don't worry about it. How about if we go back to bed and get some sleep? We can talk about this over breakfast. Maybe we can figure out what's happened here so it won't happen again. Okay?" He stood up.

"You're so calm. I'm a wreck. I don't want to cry. I cry too much these days. I'm too emotional."

"You're doing quite well, Cat, considering all that's happened. Seems that you've just had too much to deal with lately. I'm one of the things you've had to deal with, and I'm very sorry about that. You go to bed now. Close your eyes and take deep, slow breaths in and out. Think about clouds drifting slowly through the sky. You'll be asleep in a few minutes."

"Clouds? Seriously?"

"Seriously. Don't forget the breathing part."

"Okay."

As they left the bathroom, Miles clicked off the light.

Cat went into her room and turned back to him just before she closed the door.

"Clouds?"

"Clouds. Don't forget the slow, rhythmic breathing. The clouds will start singing if you breathe properly. And call me Miles, not Mr. Trevelyan. Okay?"

Cat smiled. "Okay. See you in the morning." She closed the door and returned to her bed. She didn't bother jamming the chair against her door.

Things went just as Miles had said. She closed her eyes and purposefully put thoughts of the intruder out of her mind. She began the slow breathing in and out and imagined clouds floating over the Mule Mountains of Bisbee, Arizona. She drifted off before the clouds had a chance to start singing.

* * *

Miles, on the other hand, was wide awake. After half an hour of staring at the ceiling, he turned on a small lamp, opened his laptop and wrote an email to his dad in Sussex.

Hi Dad, Just wanted you to know that I arrived safely in Bisbee, Arizona. You can find it on the map. It's a small town southeast of Tucson and really close to the U.S.-Mexico border. Very charming little town. You'd like it. Something about it reminds me of Cornwall, but with desert mountains, not the sea. That probably doesn't make any sense, does it? The weather here is great. Very sunny and warm. It's late now so I'll write more tomorrow. Love, Miles

Miles went back to bed. He wasn't any closer to sleep. His state of mind was a combination of excitement and concern. La señorita Catalina Amalia Miranda was the loveliest woman he'd met on this trip. Actually, she was one of the loveliest women he'd ever met anywhere. She wasn't really a conventional beauty, nor would she stand out in a crowd. She was so little that she'd never make it as one of those tall models he saw on television striding down the fashion runway in London. She would, however, fit right under his chin.

Yes, she was lovely. So Mexican. So American. So Borderlands. Yes, that was it. She was a womanly epitome of the Borderlands. Dark eyes. Lovely long dark hair. Rich soft brown skin. Full, soft red lips. Sweet, funny, and very sexy. She seemed completely unaware of her allure. Sitting in front of her in the bathroom when she tended his wound had been a delight. True, he found it amusing to think about scaring off a bandito. But the real delight was Cat herself. She had on a thin nightgown, and his eyes were on the level of her breasts as she cleaned and bandaged his scratch. Yes, delightful. But he'd kept his hands to himself, and he'd said nothing because he had promised her that he'd be a good bloke. He sighed.

Coupled with these pleasant thoughts, Miles also felt a deep concern. Why was someone breaking into Cat's home in the middle of the night? Miles was so glad he'd been there. Otherwise, she would have been all on her own to face the intruder. He would talk to her in the morning to see if they could figure out what they could do to prevent this from happening again. He most definitely wanted the lovely Cat Miranda to be safe.

Miles decided to try the breathing exercises that he'd recommended to Cat. Eventually, he, too, fell asleep.

2 MILES

As usual, Cat woke up at first light. A friend had teased her once and said she must be the child of peasant farmers to wake up so early. She had no idea if she was descended from farmers. She knew only about her mother's family. Her mother came from a long line of hardworking Mexicans and Mexican Americans. They tended shops and worked on cars and cooked meals and ran cattle and sold things in the market. Cat's mom was first in the family to go to college, graduate and then become a nurse. But Cat knew almost nothing about her father.

She stretched out in bed and listened to morning sounds. The house was quiet though she could hear a bird in the mesquite tree near her window. The song sounded like a phainopepla, a type of flycatcher that looked very much like a cardinal but black, not red. She could hear Inca doves, too. No sounds came from Luis's room. Her guest – she frowned slightly at the idea of Miles Trevelyan as a B&B guest – must still be asleep. She didn't really know what to do about his presence. He seemed nice enough, and he was nice to look at. But she had plenty to deal with right now, and a guest was a bit much. Time to rise and shine. She jumped out of bed and went to the bathroom.

Cat looked in the bathroom mirror. She noticed dark shadows under her brown eyes, and her shoulder-length dark hair was a mess. She looked tired and stressed already, and it was only early morning. She sighed, tied her hair with a band and pinned it up. She stepped into the shower. The warm water felt great. After her shower, she dressed in her favorite winter outfit, black leggings, a t-shirt, and a thigh-length, knitted pull-over sweater in a rich magenta color. Her favorite black half-boots went on her feet.

Fifteen minutes later, Cat was downstairs in her tiny kitchen making coffee. She could hear stirring upstairs. While she waited for the coffee, she wandered from the back of the building, where the kitchen was located, to the art gallery in the main part of the building. The gallery had been created by Luis from a large, two-story house that had existed on the property for nearly eighty years. He had hollowed out most of the ground-floor living and dining area to make as large a gallery space as possible. There was a smaller room off the main gallery that he used for storage. The back of the old home still had the tiny kitchen with a small table only big enough for two or three people to sit and eat. Out the back door, the door Miles had entered the previous night, there was a *portál*, an attached covered porch that ran the length of the back of the house. A larger table and several chairs were there ready if she wanted to entertain guests. There was also an old wooden swing on a stand under the porch, too. She and Luis used to sit on it together and take turns reading to each other.

The thought crossed Cat's mind that, if she really wanted to turn the upstairs into a B&B, she was going to have to do some serious remodeling and probably build onto the old structure. But really, there just wasn't enough room for her to live here and have a B&B, too. She wondered what Luis had in mind when he considered opening a B&B. The idea was overwhelming, but then it seemed to Cat that nearly everything was overwhelming these days. Caring for her dying brother, escaping Phoenix, escaping her ex-husband Al, starting a new life here in her childhood home of Bisbee. It was a lot. The idea of a B&B seemed too much right now. Maybe there was something else going on that she didn't know about. But she would never know now what Luis had been thinking because he wasn't here to tell her. Miles Trevelyan seemed like a nice guy, but he was a real inconvenience at the moment.

And there was that second intruder last night. She cringed. Something else to worry about.

She walked slowly around the perimeter of the gallery, the Sonoran Art Gallery. She liked the name. It was a cross-border kind of name that reflected the Sonoran Desert region she lived in. She knew that Luis had a dream of building Bisbee into an art center on the level of Santa Fe, New Mexico. He wanted to give local artists in the Bisbee area a chance to show and sell their art. He hoped to bring artists in from across the border, too. His dream was to make it a real Borderlands gallery. More than anything, Luis wanted local artists to prosper. Now that dream had become Cat's dream, too.

Cat could smell the coffee so she returned to the kitchen. She started breakfast – a typical and very simple Mexican breakfast. She cooked eggs and fried potatoes and wondered if her guest liked Mexican food. She found some *salsa verde* in an unopened glass jar on the shelf, and a chunk of cheese in the fridge. In the freezer, she found some frozen tortillas, thawed them out, and began frying them on the griddle. Not the best tortillas in the world, but better than no tortillas at all. She was just glad that she'd stopped off at the market for the eggs, potatoes, and coffee the night before. Going grocery shopping was on the list for today. She could hear Miles coming down the stairs. He appeared carrying a small backpack.

"Good morning," Cat said with a brief smile. "As I mentioned last night, I don't have any of that dark breakfast tea that you English dudes like to drink. I only have coffee."

"No problem. I like coffee, too."

In the light of day, Cat thought Miles looked different than he had last night. He was rested, or at least more than he had been. He seemed quite relaxed, like a man on vacation. He was dressed in jeans, a blue flannel shirt over a blue t-shirt, and hiking boots. His strawberry blond hair was tousled, and the stubble on his face was gone. His blue eyes were shining, and he was smiling. Cat couldn't help but notice that Miles Trevelyan was an attractive man. She gestured for him to sit down.

"The food isn't great, but it's better than nothing. I'm going shopping today."

He scooped both the eggs and fried potatoes onto a tortilla, then smeared the *salsa verde* on everything. "What's this?" he pointed to the cheese.

"That's *quesillo*. It's Oaxacan cheese."

Miles cut off a bite and tasted it. "Ummm....that's good." He turned up the lower end of his full tortilla to prevent anything from falling out of the bottom then neatly rolled it up. Half of the breakfast burrito went directly into his mouth.

"Where did you learn how to properly roll up a tortilla?"

He swallowed the first mouthful. "In Texas. McAllen to be exact. My first stop on my tour. First task. Learn how to make a proper burrito."

Cat watched him eat. He was an enthusiastic eater. He was rolling a second tortilla now, and he had cut off more of the *quesillo*. She was still working on her first burrito when he finished his second.

"This is so good." He smiled. "Thank you for breakfast."

Cat nodded. "I was wondering if you could tell me more about yourself and how it is that you came to rent a room from my brother. You know, we shared everything about our business plans. He never mentioned a bed and breakfast."

"I could be wrong about the B&B. It's possible that he was just renting the room out as a one-time deal. The B&B notion came from one of the people who directed me to Luis. She told me that a lot of people in Bisbee have opened B&Bs and rent out rooms during your busy season here. Maybe I just jumped to the conclusion that Luis was thinking of that. I don't really know for sure. After I wired the money to his attorney, Luis gave me a key to the back door and told me to text him a day or two before I was to arrive. I followed his instructions although I never got an answer to my text."

"What's this about wiring money to his lawyer?"

"Yes, I paid in advance. The lawyer's name is...," he hesitated. "It's Jeremy something. I forget his last name. It's a Spanish family name."

"Jeremy Flores?"

"That's right. Jeremy Flores. He didn't tell you?"

"I just came home to Bisbee. I haven't had a chance to see Jeremy. But I'll go see him this morning and find out about this. And there may be other things I need to know about, too." Cat frowned. "How much did Luis charge you?"

"About three hundred and eighty-five British pounds," Miles smiled. "Five hundred U.S. dollars."

"Wow. That's a good deal. Two weeks for five hundred dollars. Why did he give you such a good deal?"

"I think your brother liked me. He wanted to talk about the history of the Borderlands. He liked it that I am a scholar."

Cat nodded. "That sounds just like my brother. He liked to read, and he loved history. I think maybe Luis gave you a good deal in exchange for good conversation."

"The good deal also includes breakfast."

"*What*? Breakfast, too?" Cat snorted. "I'm not much of a cook. Are you ready for a bowl of cereal or eggs and tortillas every morning while you're here?"

"No problem. I like to cook. I'll make breakfast for us, m'lady."

"Why do you say that 'm'lady' thing?"

Miles shrugged his shoulders. "I'm an Englishman. And you seem like a lady to me." He reached for a third tortilla.

Cat couldn't help herself. She was surprised and unaccountably pleased to hear him say this.

"So you're working on a book? What's the book about?"

"About four hundred pages." He smiled.

Cat rolled her eyes. "You're such a smart ass." She couldn't help but smile a little.

"I'm a witty Englishman, not an American smart ass."

"Want to try again? What's your book about?" she repeated.

"My book will be about the U.S.-Mexico Borderlands. I started out studying the history of Mexico, specifically the post-1910 Revolutionary period. That was the subject of my dissertation and my first book. That led me to learn about a lot of interesting events on both sides of the border. From there, I became more and more interested in the entire U.S.-Mexico Borderlands, its history, culture, and the people who live here. I have found that the Borderlands are unique — not really American, not really Mexican."

"That's true."

He stared at his empty plate. "I probably ate too much. I like Mexican food. In my opinion, the food here is better than in Texas. Tucson has some really good restaurants."

"Yes, Sonoran cuisine is better than Tex-Mex. Everyone knows that except the Texans. Want more coffee?"

"Yes, please. Then I'd like to ask you some questions. We need to figure out why someone wants to get into your gallery and your living quarters."

"Like Englishmen who get really fabulous deals on a room and breakfast for a couple of weeks?"

"That's your good bloke. What about the bad bloke dressed all in black who broke in upstairs last night? Any ideas about who he was and what he wanted?"

"No," Cat frowned. "I have no idea. We've never had a break-in here."

"He may have thought that no one was here."

"Possibly. I just returned yesterday. My car is at the truck rental place. He probably saw the moving van outside but figured it was just parked there overnight."

"Do you think he wanted to steal some art?"

Cat shrugged her shoulders. "If that's the case, why not break in downstairs? He could have come in the back door. I doubt if it's that hard to break open. The kitchen windows also would be easy to get into, I think."

"Let's look in your gallery. Perhaps you can show me what's there."

They both rose and went into the main gallery. Paintings were on all four walls and there were a couple of sculptures on pedestals. A glass case against the back wall held some unique, original jewelry pieces that looked more like sculpture than jewelry.

Miles stopped in front of a painting that dominated one wall. At eight feet tall and five feet wide, the painting dwarfed all other paintings in the gallery. It had diagonal stripes in shades of gray across the canvas with three huge pairs of human lips in black topped by three additional images of lips in red and orange, ready to give someone a kiss. Miles looked closer at the placard attached to the wall. It read: "Kissed." Then the artist's name. Jax Beringer.

"The title is 'Kissed'?"

"That's right."

"What does it mean? Why is it so big?"

"I don't know," Cat said. "Luis hung it not long before I came back here to take care of him. Luis said he put it up for gallery visitors to see the latest Jax Beringer painting. Beringer is an up-and-coming artist. Luis sold a lot of his paintings, mainly online through our website."

"So Jax Beringer lives in Bisbee?"

"Yes. I only met him once and just briefly. I thought he was kind of a *pendejo*. Oh, do you know that word? You speak Spanish?"

"Yes, I speak a little. That word means 'arsehole,' right?"

Cat nodded. "Luis introduced us one weekend when I came home for a visit. Honestly, within five minutes of meeting me, he was hitting on me and making sexually suggestive comments." She wrinkled up her nose. "He was really arrogant. He seemed to think he was God's gift to women."

"So Luis represented Beringer mainly for financial purposes? Not because they were friends?"

"That's correct. I don't think Beringer was such a dick at first, but he got more demanding all the time."

"Do you have more of his paintings? Are they the most valuable of all the artists you represent?"

"Yes and yes. His paintings have greater financial value than any of our other artists. There are a couple of smaller ones on that wall." She gestured behind her. "And we have at least ten in storage. Maybe more…."

About the Author

C.J. Shane is an artist and writer based in Tucson, Arizona, USA. She is the author of the Letty Valdez mystery series, the Cat Miranda mystery series, and the Iron Horse mystery series. Learn more at cjshane.com